Praise for Eugen Bacon's Work

"Eugen Bacon is a master of using bold, evocative prose to guide the reader through a uniquely speculative world. It's clear the author has selected each word with great care, artfully arranging them throughout the narrative with an almost musical quality that begs to be read aloud in order to fully experience Bacon's own brand of sound magic." —**P.A. Cornell**, Nebula finalist author of "Once Upon a Time at the Oakmont"

"Complex, earnest, and striking, Bacon's impeccable work is sure to blow readers away."—*Publishers Weekly*

"*The Nga'phandileh Whisperer* by Eugen Bacon is bursting with imagination, culture, magic, and the mystique of distant worlds. This enchanting yarn blends science fiction, fantasy, and horror to create a beautiful and timeless song." —**Pedro Iniguez**, Bram Stoker Award® winner and author of *Echoes and Embers: Speculative Stories*

"Bacon's work is staggeringly good" —*Booklist*

"*The Nga'phandileh Whisperer* is mythic and ancient, feverish and insistent, lyrical and atmospheric, eerie yet enchanting—an enticingly strange exploration of the power of sound by a poetic storyteller." —**Ai Jiang**, Nebula and Bram Stoker and Hugo Award finalist author of *A Palace Near the Wind* and *Linghun*

"Bacon's fiction playfully defamiliarizes how we understand humanity, gender, and the everyday, by freely imagining alternative worlds and possibilities, with stories that are truly speculative and invite us to see our own world with new eyes." —**Otherwise Motherboard, Fellowship Committee**

"Bacon takes readers into a dark speculative world. Her use of surrealism to explore culture, mythology, climate change and diversity, among other themes, is evocative, compelling and lyrical."
—*Weekend Australian*

"Bacon packs a great deal into a deceptively slim volume." —*Cosmic Roots & Eldritch Shores*

"Bacon is at her best when spinning yarns of fantastic creatures and otherworldly beings, many of which derive from African or Australian traditions."—*BSFA Review*

The Nga'phandileh Whisperer

A Sauútiverse Novella

Eugen Bacon

ISBN: 979-8-9914419-2-6 (trade paper)
ISBN: 979-8-9914419-4-0 (hardcover)
ISBN: 979-8-9914419-3-3(ebook: ePub)
Library of Congress Control Number: 2025933425

First printing edition: September 2, 2025
Published by Stars and Sabers Publishing in the United States of America.
Cover Artwork: Stephen Embleton | https://stephen.embleton.co.za/
Cover Design and Layout: Dash Creative
Edited by Jendia Gammon and Gareth L. Powell
Proofreading and Interior Layout by Scarlett R. Algee

https://www.starsandsabers.com/

The Nga'phandileh Whisperer

~

Zezépfeni is a rapidly orbiting planet in the Sauútiverse, and experiences rapid seasonal changes, meteor strikes, and a lingering threat of the Nga'phandileh, beings of unreality. It is a difficult world to inhabit, fortified with technology and magic. This story is set in New Inku'lulu, a Zezépfeni lookalike space outpost— here, Guardians of the tower use special prayer to secure a part of the undisclosed Hogiiri Hile Halah, the bounding wall protecting the federation of planets from the Nga'phandileh.

~

The Nga'phandileh Whisperer

Prologue

This is a story about family and Guardianship. You know that story? The one about knowing with diligence what to guard against. That year you were sick, Chant'L, you'd just turned four maybe five yourself, spent day after day in bed—all those days. You were shedding weight like a once-swollen bag of dried millet now with a hole in it. Someone must have cast an evil sound on you. All meaning was just about broken and you could not look at a bed one more time. Baba—who told you stories about how New Inku'lulu came to be, a space outpost in the image of Zezépfeni—took you to see the uroh-ogi, the healer named Mkha'lingalinga, same one who strode bare-toed and put nothing to cover her chest, even as she shone light waves, aimed at you with laser rays and put nanomaterial into sweetened yams and cassava to supplement your diet. She chewed and spat to make rubs and tonics, and something must have worked because it gave you a second wind, too much colour in your bones.

On a short dark night, you cut a pole from the back garden. Carved it with a bread knife, polished it with sand cloth and wedged it on the hinges of your bedchamber door. All this to do exercises butt-naked and on your own like a night runner. Mama and Baba woke up to this giant thud, rushed because a beast was killing you, only to find
that you had slipped
put a dent in the
sapele mahogany
where you'd
banged it
with your
head.

1.

ziiiiiiiiiiiiiiiiiiiiiiiiiiiiiiiiiiiiiiiiiiiiiiiiiiiiiiiiiiiiiiiiiiiiiiiiiiiiiiiiiiiiiiiiiiiiiiiiiii iiiiiiiiiiiiiiiiiiiiiiiiiiiiiiiiii

biiiiiiiiiiiiiiiiiiiiiiiiiiiiiiiiiiiiiiiiiiiiiiiiiiiiiiiiiiiiiiiiiiiiiiiiiiiiiiiiiiiiiiiiiiiiiiiiiii iiiiiiiiiiiiiiiiiiiiiiiiiiiiiiiiii

tuuuuuuuuuuuuuuuuuuuuuuuuuuuuuuuuuuuuuuuuuuuuuuuuuuuuuuuuuuuuuuuu uuuuuuuuuuuuuuuuuuuuuu

That's the sound of incoherence. The mindless cry of what is trapped within the wall—the Hogiiri Hile Halah. That's the name of the wall.

The Hogiiri Hile Halah offers, and it takes. What it gives is disarray, because what does the sound even mean? But the pulse inside the wall is not as mindless as you think. It's a hum, a buzz that overwhelms the need for sensibility.

Buzzzzzzzzzzzzzzzzzzzzzzzzzzz.

It's a throb you feel too late. A rhythm *they* feel too late. And who are y*ou*? Who are *they*? It's everybody. You, them, they. Everyone but the Guardians, the protectors. Aren't you one of them? A curious child of Sector Z in the elite district of New Inku'lulu, and here you are. Shedding caution and slipping, without warning, your flat-booted feet stepping into the sacred courtyard of the Tower of Guardians.

A layered buzz of a jillion hearts zings in an echo entrapped within the invisible wall. It quietens at your approach, such hush— you can hear your own heart beating.

Bom.

Bom.

Bombombombombom.

In the deadest of silence, just then, the wall's buzz resurrects itself. At first it's gentle. So soft its calling out to you, to them, it nudges you, them, to step forward. To listen, please listen.

Bombombombombom, goes your heart.

You lean your ear towards the luring, you know how?

Buzzzzzzzzzzzzzzzzzzzzzzzzz, it says. Buzz, says the luring.

The sound wills you with a gobbling need, one that tells you, that *insists*, and you know you must touch it. Touch the wall, please touch the wall, it begs—even though you cannot see it, the desire so great. A surging need unravels your being, and your hand draws closer, closer still. Your fingers twitch, curl back into themselves, as if no. But you can't help it. You cannot help but do the touching.

And when you do—

Even with sound magic.

The jolt from touching the wall kicks you inside out. It knocks gale out of you, leaves your ears whistling, every inch of your body scorching. Then a cold impassiveness gulps you, until finally a giddiness overwhelms your mind.

The first time it happened, buzzzzzzzzzzzzzzzzzzzzzzzzzzz, you threw up. Literally. Yellows, greens, pinks and oranges. They fell out of your mouth in all bitterness, lumps of unsavoury coagulation far different from your dinner that exited your throat. They hurled themselves out with such punishing, you thought you would die, and then die, and die more still until only empty hacking remained. It collapsed your body, emptied it of pumpkin, spice, cassava, groundnuts and leaves simmered through dusk in a clay-bottomed pot all charred and hungry with the orange and blue licks of a three-hearth flame. Just like Mama's old-fashioned kitchenette, her *new and old* under a louvered-roof pergola. Fancy that—a kitchen in its sole self on three fat-bottomed stones in a swanky pergola.

Damn.

Buzzzzzzzzzzzzzzzzzzzzzzzzzzz.

You feel weak, spent. It's as if an old, fat baobab has given up the ghost and crashed on top of you, never minding its weight and the squishing of what you might next become. And that's what you feel *with* sound magic. Imagine how it is, what one feels without magic, and they do.

When the foolish ones touch the wall without sound magic—

It's not the Hogiiri Hile Halah that takes. What snatches lurks inside the wall.

Buzzzzzzzzzzzzzzzzzzzzzzzzzzz.

You know about it and only because Kari'bu, not Mama, damn you, Mama, for not telling, it was Kari'bu who told you about the planes of existence. How the Nga'phandileh lurk in a dark place, trapped with sound magic inside the wall.

You've always loved stories, legends, myths and ballads mostly. You know how there are always folktales about why not? Why nobody should ever do this or that. They are the kind of folklore *every* mother uses to warn their wayward child. Never cross a lizard with naked feet. Never look at a black kunkun—what a ferocious cat! You must never look it in the eye. It's a story the Guardians repeat with the same outcomes of unheeding. Not about crossing lizards or looking dooming kunkuns in the eye. The Guardians' warning is better than this. And it stretches beyond New Inku'lulu, let alone Sector Z.

But still.

Folk enter the courtyard. Because why? Because why not. Think back to when you were a child, even now in the age of your own self. When did stories ever dissuade anybody?

You fear the most for Mau'aa. Every day you wake up from a bad dream with a cold sweat. And those dreams are *nasty*. So foul, you wouldn't command them on anybody. And folk always die in the same manner: with the deepest fear. What if, dear Mother, creator Goddess, your blessed heart Mau'aa finds her way to the courtyard? That is your biggest fear, Chant'L. That Mau'aa will lovingly, foolishly, whichever-ly, that she might unwittingly reach the Hogiiri Hile Halah and touch it.

And then what?

Your dread about this possibility is a tomb. It's a cold, dark coffin packed inside a small space, yet you're alive inside. It's the sound of a fist of soil from a loved one sodden in tears, and it thuds on your casket, and nothing can sew back the pieces of their wrecked heart already gathering hatred against the world, and you.

Hearts.

A stopped heart on cold grey skin is harsh to witness. But this—

And it's not even a heart.

What you're looking at is more cruel than a cold grey heart of lost love.

The still body speaks the terror of its death. Your gaze follows fingers clasping for the ravenous buzz throwing itself against the wall, too keen for human touch. You study with inquisitiveness, loathing and perhaps some attraction the deep black cavern charcoaled into a fossil. That's all that is left of the intruding man or woman's stomach.

What manner of intruder alert—as in, don't do it—will work with efficacy, if not this most horrible death? But the Guardians will not parade the bodies as they ought to.

You wonder what brought these intruders to the wall, and if they found what it was they were looking for. You ponder the yawning mouth, jaws widened in a quietened screech—

Is it a cry of sadness, terror or joy?

You consider this for a long time. Unable to find answers, and exhausted of questions, you shape your mouth and slip your fingers in, just before your tongue. You take a deep breath, pause, then sound the whistle.

It feels like forever but only takes a moment. A rhythmic clapping in a rise and fall accompanying a chant-filled harmony tells you that your alarm has been heard.

The Guardians are coming.

2.

Khwa'ra. It is acquired.
Ya'yn. It is uttered.
Ra'kwa. It is released.

That is the song of Our Mother. That is the tail of the Hogiiri Hile Halah chant, the one that cleanses the wall. You have sung it in full. Now you hum it freestyle around the corpse, careful not to touch the body because, Our Mother help us, the Nga'phandileh are cunning. Do you know about touch? Who knows what touch might do? The path it might encourage from the wall to a dead one to a live one. It could be you if you're not careful. The unsuspecting carrier from a pulsing wall through a corpse because you were foolish enough to touch.

 Khwa'ra.
  Ya'yn.
  Ra'kwa.

You hum together—you, Mwe'ra, Kari'bu, Nd'ani, Pita and Jin. They are the Guardians who made you. Mwe'ra's sound magic comes out in echo. He repeats words in an ancient tongue. A hum that goes, 'Joramjoramjora.'

Kari'bu's chant is a pleasant melody. She reminds you of Mama, her sound soft as the feathers of a baby egret. Nd'ani's—she's an angry one and you never know why. Her sound magic comes out in a grunt. Pita is a special one. His magic comes out as if he's flinging something away—but they're weak fists. You call them haymakers. As for his magic! It sounds like the cough of a sick donkey. The first time you heard it, it took everything inside you to contain the laugher. And you nearly failed to hold it in, infectious like Baba's laughter. You put a hand to your stomach, and thank Our Mother it helped. What didn't help was how Pita doubled and purpled, as he's doing now, to dispense his magic. It makes you think of a grown one pushing out an impossible fart. Jin, ah, Jin. They are doing an incredible feat, chanting as they are in that scratching noise, and inebriated as they are. Their feet are unsteady, but their magic doesn't fade.

Khwa'ra.

> *Ya'yn.*

> *Ra'kwa.*

It is acquired. It is uttered. It is released.

Your together magic, the potency of this group magic, is overwhelming.

The charred body of the dead one fades in an explosion and a giant smoke. Exorcised with your collective hum to free its soul from bad spirits so it can make it to Eh'wauizo.

Now the rest of the ritual must begin, and this is the part you don't like every much. As it stands, someone must sound the horn and run the streets on bare feet. The blown horn will rouse the sleeping people of Sector Z in New Inku'lulu, the Zezépfeni look-alike outpost. In this elite space station that's home to the Guardians of the tower, the horn will announce that someone has breached something—nobody cares what. All tradition demands is that, where there is a breach to the tower of Guardians, a barter be made to appease the gods.

No, not again.

Mwe'ra, Kari'bu, Nd'ani, Pita and Jin turn in unison and look at you in that telling way. Mwe'ra, being the elder guardian, wears the arrogance of a leader who knows his time is coming to an end, but dares anyone to take it from him. Pita has lips of fatefulness stuck in a forever downturn, and they are pouting at you now. Drunken Jin regards you cockeyed with the uncertainty of sunken eyes and unsteady feet, and you fear they might collapse any instant now. Nd'ani glares at you with the fierceness of a gaze that says you've wronged her, even though you know in all manner and sincerity that you haven't.

It's only Kari'bu who smiles encouragement. But you know better than to trust that smile. It's the kind that assures you'll be fine whether you believe it or not, and you just know you won't be fine.

You're the youngest and fastest in the tower—they all know this. You know this. Somehow this seems to dispel any argument, or insistence from you for a reason that feeds this dynamic.

Kari'bu hands you the blowing horn. 'You do it, Chant'L.'

Resolutely, you clasp it.

3.

Now the blowing horn is a funny thing, not the 'ha-ha kind'. You know, as anybody would, that it's deadly to carry about the hone of atonement in the randomness of New Inku'lulu's weather. If you stumbled on slippery road and fell on its sharpest nose—

A drizzle is just starting as you peddle off with unwillingness. You have considered and abandoned, yet again, the use of sound magic. You know how you can so easily think yourself to a destination? Will the rowdy weather halt with a thought? But—for this diplomatic mission—you're forbidden to use magic in the bidding of the wall for the purpose of appeasement.

Empowered, the people know this. And your inability at this time to use magic fills them with vindictiveness. Their belligerence that comes with any imbalance of power grows thorns. And though one of them may have wronged the system with invasion—this is all they need to know, little specifics—they stay venomous. This is what the bright metallic sound of a horn induces in them. Specifically, when the blowing is metered out just before dawn, way before the two suns, Zuúv'ah and Juah-āju, have considered to emerge in their yellowest splendour.

You remember how the first time in your newness you blew the dastardly horn and only a broken sound petered out. It woke no one. The shame of it. But now you have mastered the unpleasant loudness that yields swift results, and you must be quick about it.

Pitter patter pitter patter, the sound of your feet. You stamp across the main streets of Sector Z, spreading terrible noise with your ghastly horn.

Lights snap on.

As you race past them, you wonder what it must feel to live inside those rock houses burrowed in hillocks, most of them radiant roofed on weather-resistant honeycomb domes in neat cocoons. Other residential homes are shaped like wings of giant birds shimmering in dusk's short spell. They have curves, lines and perforations in their vessel shapes with eyes and noses torn into concrete and steel, and they remind you of interplanetary shuttles with their smooth noses and tapered bodies lifting for the sky. It is impossible to imagine that, once, Sector Z and the whole of New Inku'lulu housed only thatch-roofed mud huts. Technology has changed everything, except the babies who startle awake and wail out loud.

You stay away from the roads that will take you to Mama. She gave you away.

'Go easy with that blasted horn, you chekele'le turd!' a different mother yells, and you know she's wishing you would, indeed, transmute into the faeces of the greedy, short hind-legged beast. Is that what Mama considered before she stepped into herself?

More lights snap on.

'Get away from here, you thrice-chewed, bandy-legged, half-blind cockerel!' another cry from inside a techno-savvy house.

If there's one thing to appreciate—if at all it's possible to appreciate it—it's the new colourfulness of the curses people hurl your way:

'Bum-birthed, spindle-legged offshoot of a sodomising tikolokolo!' Not the spirit gremlin!

'Inside-out, skinless, uselessly fireless dragon-no!'

'Disowned, illicit bastard of a gummy-toothed mamba'ba!'

'Shat from the smelly buttocks of a rotted impundu-pudu!' Now you're the refuse of a lightning bird.

'Bed-wetting lousen toad! Woken by your own fart-filled, disease-infused hallucinations?'

Nyaaauuuuu! Someone throws a kunkun at you. The ferocious cat lands, claws out, on your shoulder and you both yowl. It hisses and scatters away. You have time in a moment of sanity to consider it might be a tamed one, that perhaps it simply fell by itself from a window or a ledge, angered, frightened or disconcerted by your ridiculous horning.

It is raining full pelt now.

A crowd of unkempt youths fattens from nowhere and starts chasing you. You're grateful for the flat boots, but fear you might trip on the flowing sarong of your vest dress. But it is how it is. It happens like this all the time. And you hate it, dear Mother, you hate it. The people of Sector Z in New Inku'lulu hate it too, the ritual, not the insults—they seem to thrive on those. But the ritual is a ritual, and it must be done. You cannot use magic, even if those youths catch you, and so you run as if your life depended on it, and it does. All that running and still blowing the ghastly horn, that is a feat no one seems to appreciate.

Only later, in the safety of the tower, might you consider the people's belligerence. Perhaps it reflects their true relationship with the Guardians. That they harbour a passive aggressiveness that manifests itself with the blowing of the horn. And that's what adds to the complexity of it. Because, inside all that mistrust, there's also a trust relationship. All the people need to know is that something, a secret something in the tower, has been breached—but what exactly? They don't care to know. All they know is that one family will wake to one of its own forever missing, taken by sound magic. What again, exactly? Who cares.

They don't know about the wall and its secret of the Nga'phandileh. It's only visible to the Guardians. People trust enough in the breach, without seeing it, announced through the horn, to atone for it. How impossible is this? Yet it is possible.

Perhaps their intensity to hurt you is to show you what else is impossible. You don't want to think what they might do if they catch you like this, unmagicked. You fly into the courtyard, just barely, all slippery from the rain.

The horn clatters from your hands, having accomplished its purpose.

4.

Mwe'ra, Kari'bu, Nd'ani, Pita and Jin—none of them are there for the next phase of the people's atonement. There's only you.

You stand drenched by the gate in the outer courtyard, but *inside* the wall. Now they cannot harm you. One by one, sometimes in twos, they appear—transformed. You'd think it wasn't them maddened with killing. Them that wanted to reach into your skin and rip out your bones. Their approach now is entreating within the tower's boundaries.

'Tomorrow belongs to the people.' They offer customary greeting.

'We prepare for it this moment,' you reply.

'Tomorrow belongs to the people.'

'We prepare for it this moment.' Over and over, your response to everyone who offers greeting, then a gift.

Without magic, you cannot tell which were the ones who hurled at you eggs, potatoes, insults and stones.

And just like that it's dawn under a white, scorching sun. The outer courtyard is overflowing with gifts: mats, baskets—some laden with eggs, normal fowl ones, not the giant ones that you get from ndege'ndege nests. More gifts: cowrie shells, dried meat, sweet bananas, millet, rice. Someone has offered up a fully grown horned nguwe'we, and it is honking its outrage, dare you touch it. You make a mental note that you will make a good dinner of it soon.

'Tomorrow belongs to the people,' a young woman says.

The world stops for a moment. It's Mau'aa.

'We prepare for it this moment,' you manage to say.

(((

You were children before the world forced you to grow. You played together, picked pebbles by their shape and colour, spat on them and polished them with the palms of your hands until the pebbles shone like Vuiili-ki and Vuiili-ku, the spirit moons of Wiimb-ó.

You dreamt together from early on, those years as young'uns back then, floated together on stars.

One day you said, 'I want to become a guardian.'

'And live in the tower?' she asked.

'Yes.'

'Be celibate all the time?'

'Yes.'

You weren't serious then. You didn't think it would actually happen like it eventually did.

She said, 'It's chill.'

But you knew from the way she said it that it was sizzler all the way. There was nothing chill about it.

(((

You look at her now, the young woman she has become. She's related through a great, great anko to Jin, but resembles nothing of their disproportion between nose and lips, eyes and ears. Forehead arriving first, bones jutting out where they shouldn't. That's Jin.

Mau'aa is nothing like Jin. She has the face of a petal. Her hair twined in rowdy curls falling down her chest. She hands you a black pearl bracelet and looks at you sweetly, the night in her eyes calling, calling. She is moondust.

Moondust.

That's all you're thinking.

Even as she is donating your gift. You look at it, numb, as if unseeing.

She has brought the bracelet you gave her. The one that came from planet Órino-Rin but you bought it from a merchant in the local market.

From the heart wrench you feel, she could well have donated all your livers. She couldn't say it any louder for you both. She is divorcing herself from you.

You ought not to care, but you do.

5.

Khwa'ra.
  Ya'yn.
    Ra'kwa.

Mwe'ra, Kari'bu, Nd'ani, Pita and Jin—they are the Guardians who made you.

Taught you about what it means to be celibate: madness. Reminded you not to care about the likes of Mau'aa: no luck. Taught you to protect Zezépfeni with an assemblage of kindred magic because a perilously-close threat lurking inside the wall: now, about that...

Whatever happens, Mau'aa or not, you're sworn to do everything to keep the beings of unreality from leaking into your reality.

This, right now, means accepting a 'donated' gift that massacres you to take it.

6.

ziiiiiiiiiiiiiiiiiiiiiiiiiiiiiiiiiiiiiiiiiiiiiiiiiiiiiiiiiiiiiiiiiiiiiiiiiiiiiiiiiiiiiiiiiiiiiiiiiiiiiiiiiiiiiii iiiiiiiiiiiiiiiiiiiiiiiiiiiiiiiii
biiiiiiiiiiiiiiiiiiiiiiiiiiiiiiiiiiiiiiiiiiiiiiiiiiiiiiiiiiiiiiiiiiiiiiiiiiiiiiiiiiiiiiiiiiiiiiiiiiiiiiiiiiiiiiiiiiiiiii iiiiiiiiiiiiiiiiiiiiiiiiiiiiiiii
tuuuuuuuuuuuuuuuuuuuuuuuuuuuuuuuuuuuuuuuuuuuuuuuuuuuuuuuuuuuuuuuuuu uuuuuuuuuuuuuuuuuuuuu

The Hogiiri Hile Halah is now appeased.

You cannot help but wonder if another fool will touch the wall without magic.

They better not!

Dear Mother, you silently pray. Please keep Mau'aa away, furthest away from the wall.

It's times like this that you wish sound magic exorcism didn't explode the dead ones in a puff of giant smoke, then nothing. You wish they stayed whole in gnarled forms you could display, impaled on stakes for the whole of Sector Z to witness.

Let the child touch a hot coal. Isn't that the best warning?

As if.

Would seeing gnarled, impaled bodies discourage the curious from tumbling uninvited to meet the deadly intensity entrapped inside the wall?

You know it won't.

ziiiiiiiiiiiiiiiiiiiiiiiiiiiiiiiiiiiiiiiiiiiiiiiiiiiiiiiiiiiiiiiiiiiiiiiiiiiiiiiiiiiiiiiiiiiiiiiiiiiiiiiiiiiii iiiiiiiiiiiiiiiiiiiiiiiiiiiiiiiii
biiiiiiiiiiiiiiiiiiiiiiiiiiiiiiiiiiiiiiiiiiiiiiiiiiiiiiiiiiiiiiiiiiiiiiiiiiiiiiiiiiiiiiiiiiiiiiiiiiiiiiiiiiiiiiiiiiiiiii iiiiiiiiiiiiiiiiiiiiiiiiiiiiiiiiiii
tuuuuuuuuuuuuuuuuuuuuuuuuuuuuuuuuuuuuuuuuuuuuuuuuuuuuuuuuuuuuuuuuuu uuuuuuuuuuuuuuuuuuuuuuuuuuuu.

This sound is not from the wall. It's right between your ears, and you hear it all the time. It's there as you go about your chores. Buzzzzzzzzzzzzzzzzzzzzzzz.

Buzz, says the luring.

You try to ignore it, succeed best as you can. You continue—
—sweeping, scrubbing, stir-frying, weeding.
Buzzzzzzzzzzzzzzzzzzzzzzzzzz.

You have a name for it—the sound inside your head. You call it snakes, leaves, bees, bells and beasts. And this is perturbing because you have a terror of snakes. The last place you want to find one, let alone many, is in your head. You try to stay quiet so it can sleep. On days like this, especially after the wall is disturbed, the snakes, leaves, bees, bells and beasts won't let you be. You hear them, loud as ailment. They fly, crawl, shuffle, vibrate inside the wall, inside your head. Hissing, crinkling, humming, tinkling, howling.

You shouldn't be here. Not alone like this. Too near the wall.

You shouldn't have stepped through the techno trapdoor that takes you out to the Hogiiri Hile Halah, the invisible wall that trembles, pulses, buzzes, hisses and snaps. It's a wall that calls out to your sound magic, and you're not sure you like it—the wall, the magic, or your stepping out.

What you know is an addiction. A deadly addiction.

Mama once joked about it without knowing what she was joking about. She said you were born with Mothersound. She didn't know then, or now, how close she was in this reasoning. You didn't tell her how a buzz enters your head and it's always there until it isn't. Mama only said it about the Mothersound because of your gift.

How you can traffic yourself in a blink, simply using a thought. You think of a place, and you're there. Wait, there's more. Like how the weather listens when you chant. As if that's not enough, you can bend and transform things. Camouflage them with illusion, and people trust what they see, even if it isn't. Their eyes tell them a lamp is a lamp. A pot is a pot. A protea is a protea. They never doubt to think that a lamp might be a sheaf of grass. And a pot might be a rake. And a protea might be a kunkun turd. That a coconut loaf might be a toad.

The sound has always been in your head.

You remember it as far back as recollection takes you. It's an intimate knowing that's not always a buzz. The speed, depth and intensity of the hissing, whistling, ringing or roaring varies with your mood. Truth is, you don't know whether the sound makes the mood, or the mood makes the sound.

What you do know is that the wall makes it *more*—the sound becomes bigger, more entrancing. Hypnotic. Remember how Mama said you're unpredictable, but are you?

Now here you are. Hesitant around the wall you shouldn't be near, but not keeping distance from it. You wish you'd told Baba about your secret. Those many years back when you acted out in angriness, and it disappointed him. How his kind face wore hurt. You should have told him it wasn't you. That it was the snakes, the leaves, the bees, bells and beasts between your ears. You should have told him that, on bad nights, beasts bellowed and kept you from sleep. That sometimes they made you sick, and you refused to eat food—like how you did when you were a baby. Mama told you this story, how it baffled her that you ate so poorly, then so greedily as if eating for a crowd, at intervals.

'If I didn't know any better, I'd say you're possessed with majini,' she always said. You never saw how you could have demons.

7.

But, whether or not you were possessed by majini as Mama might have thought, first you were a child. You remember the tiny room with its cosy colours. The walls were bright and friendly. A musical mount with mobile arms blinked with dimmed lights and held hand-carved gremlins. The toys were big-eyed hybrids, or you could describe them now as human-looking with the pointy ears of a kunkun, a feral cat. You quickly mastered motor skills, and the toys rattled when you stood holding the rails of your cot and went on tippy-toe to touch them.

You remember this one night past bedtime, Baba had already told you a folklore of the lizard who swallowed time and it was way past your sleep. But the land of the unawakened refused to grab you and you blinked dry-eyed at the white, white ceiling. Just then, the gremlins of your cot rattled, and you saw the kunkun. A real one. It was not kneading your blanket or purring as a tamed thing. It wasn't curious either. This one came slow and with purpose. It stalked across the bed, crouching, its head stretched in a hunt. It stopped, ready to pounce, feet from your face. You were so entranced, you didn't even cry.

In a blink Baba was there. In an unusual show of ferocity, he snatched the beast and squeezed it as if he would draw its innards out alive with his bare, beautiful hands. He jettisoned it towards a wall and, by some miraculous intervention and a terrible screech, the kunkun steered itself and soared out the window. Baba closed the window and looked at you with a face you'd never seen before. Even with your child eyes you saw how shaken he was, way more than you. He didn't scoop you in his arms to comfort you, or him. Instead, he faced the killing wall and sobbed. Loud, ugly sobs that filled you with curiosity, unease and such aching.

Baba, dear Baba.

He was so readable, you understood him well. 'Everyone has a purpose,' he said. 'Even you.' And he looked at you in a way that said you had destiny. Was it the same destiny that evolved the Guardians of the tower from the warriors they once were? Called themselves Jurors back then, now they're sages of peace who wield echo prayer rather than bursts of sonic disruption that cough out blood and tissue.

It is undoubtable that you have a gift, but it needs training to hone it to the power it can be. You remember the incident of the playpen when you bounced too high—perhaps you used levitation magic—and splashed to the floor. You remember how loud you shrieked, and Baba was there. Scooping you in his arms, rushing you to a basin where he dabbed at the cut on your knee with a soaped sponge. He rinsed it gently with warm water and put a paste from the medicine cupboard that held remedial artefacts stocked from the uroh-ogi, the healers. You remember the tenderness with which he put the wrap over your wound as all the while you clung to his neck as if you would kill him.

Baba chose for you to know firsthand the mystery of the black river. One day when he wasn't working as a law Maadiregi, a professional, he took you out there alone where the water roared and humped, and fell across rocks on waterfalls fiercer than the one at home. You watched the torrent from high up. There it was, nestled beneath a crag. You wove gingerly with Baba across boulders, squished over mushy grass to reach the waters below. The river looked ominous, so calm yet disquieting. It was pregnant with a beast. Baba took you in his arms and lifted you higher than his shoulders, as you shrieked your horror and glee, and he tossed you into the cold, greedy waters, thick as oil. You didn't fall like a stone, plonk straight to the bottom. Baba stood, arms folded over his solid chest, watching you with a big smile on his kindliest face. He watched as you splashed and spluttered, frightened of creatures the beast had birthed. But nothing reared from the river's bed to jaw you. No serpents wrapped around your feet and dragged you below. Finally, realising he was in no hurry to dive in and bring you ashore, you moved your hands and feet, paddled like a four-legger, all the way to safety by his feet.

As you grew older, you comprehended what you were capable of, so much more than Mama, Baba, or you imagined. Had you told him the truth, would he have taken you to an uroh-ogi for healing? But you're not sure it's a problem for a healer or for curing. You're not sure it's a problem at all.

What you know for sure is that gourds, drums, ointments, chants or sputum will not cure you. Sound magic does some curing, for a spell. The hiss, whistle, buzz, ring or roar inside your head sometimes feels like friends who quieten and listen when you do sound magic.

You hear their sound now. Buzzzzzzzzzzzzzzzzzzzzzzzzz.

But this time it's not in your head. It's inside the Hogiiri Hile Halah. The invisible wall that protects you and the people of Zezépfeni from the Nga'phandileh. The beasts of unreality whose buzz tells you not to trifle with them. They are as cunning as the Guardians fear. There's no telling what anomaly erupts when unreality invades the real world.

So, nightly, you and the rest of the Guardians keep them at bay. The union of your Hogiiri Hile Halah chant strengthens the wall. Before the chant, Mwe'ra puts ash on his forehead, then leads the prayers:

'Our Mother watches the wall grow.'

'As anything loved and counselled by Our Mother,' the rest of you intone.

'We echo the Word to strengthen the wall.'

'As anything loved and counselled by Our Mother,' you intone.

'Find the Word. Find the Voice,' says Mwe'ra.

'Khwa'ra. It is acquired.'

'Find the Word. Find the Voice,' says Mwe'ra.

'Ya'yn. It is uttered.'

'Find the Word. Find the Voice,' says Mwe'ra.

'Ra'kwa. It is released.'

'FIND THE WORD. FIND THE VOICE,' cries Mwe'ra.

'KHWA'RA. YA'YN. RA'KWA!'

8.

Ziiiiiiiiiiiiiiiiiiiiiiiiiiiiiiiiiiiiiiiiiiiiiiiiiiiiiiiiiiiiiiiiiiiiiiiiiiiiiiiiiiiiiiiiiiii iiiiiiiiiiiiiiiiiiiiiiiiiiiiiiiii
biiiiiiiiiiiiiiiiiiiiiiiiiiiiiiiiiiiiiiiiiiiiiiiiiiiiiiiiiiiiiiiiiiiiiiiiiiiiiiiiiiiiiiiiiiiiiiiiii iiiiiiiiiiiiiiiiiiiiiiiiiiiiiii
tuuuuuuuuuuuuuuuuuuuuuuuuuuuuuuuuuuuuuuuuuuuuuuuuuuuuuuuuuuuuu uuuuuuuuuuuuuuuuuuuuu
Ze are ze ze buzzzzzzzzzzzzzzzzzzzzzzzzz...

Sleep eludes you. A serpent has slipped from a log, branch, or cave and entered your brain. You feel so closely how it expands its ribs, how it breathes so deeply inside your space, and lets out a long exhalation. Tonight, it's quiet hissing. Not the rattling, the rubbing of scales that tosses and turns you dusk to dawn. You stare at the ceiling's silhouette, mirroring in your mind blinkless eyes, a writhing body, slither tracks in your head. Sometimes you can smell it, the snake. It smells of bad cucumbers, an odour that's most active at night. You hush your breathing, hope that will help it sleep. Sometimes it works.

Right now, the snake in your head is wide awake.

9.

Baba knew you were fated to become a guardian.

He sat you under the butterfly leaves of a mopane tree wearing the brightest green leaves on her boughs, or was it the tulip tree, its orange flowers just blooming? He sat or stood with you by the tulip or mopane tree, spoke in his quiet way, patiently explained in three complete words: 'Now you see.'

You didn't see, then, how Baba understood your loneliness. He saw how it was both a friend and a fiend. How it was the flicker that lit your magic, seared you whole until you felt together, no more alone, and it was an enemy, stifling you from the real world. Perhaps Baba understood aloneness because he came from a family of Maadiregi, those ones with a trade, and studied at the Mahadum of Law. But he was also gifted with the magic of weather, which made him an anomaly. Imagine how they must have heckled at him. The clever with knowledge chortling at the foolish one navel-gazing about a different kind of sound magic that was not about trade.

Perhaps it was this lonesomeness that drew him to commune with keepers of the secrets of the echo spire, those Guardians of the tower: Hulor Mwe'ra, Hulor Kari'bu, Hulor Nd'ani, Hulor Pita and Hulor Jin. He made friends of them and spent much time with the Guardians, and sometimes you resented it when he wasn't patiently coaching you, instead giving time to strangers. But were they strangers? True, they did not embrace him as a fellow guardian, though they did consult him.

Like when all the lakes and rivers dried up and the Guardians needed a special chant to squeeze out water from the earth's feet. Or like when it rained many days straight, and they sought Baba's sound magic to cut a maze of unwet where folk could find respite from furious rain. His magic was weather bound, like yours. Baba could bend the climate.

One day he said, 'Now, you see,' and you recall it vividly, because that is the day you played a cruel prank on Mama.

A part of you regrets the tricks you played back then, most of them on your mother before... before... Before the badness happened and she stepped into herself, so near yet the furthest away from you. Perhaps if you had siblings... What you needed was play and the absence of it made Mama a substitute. It didn't help that your untrained gift demanded that you be recluse until you understood to command it, lest it bring harm.

'It's a gift that arrived early,' Mama explained. 'It astonished me severely to witness it from when you were a child.'

'Like how?'

'Like how you were a bub and I put you in a cot, then I was asleep. I was lost in dreaming, and woke to find you pulling at my breast, having transported your baby self from your cot to my great big bed. That was cheeky.'

She knuckled your head in jest.

You laughed, the memory of your ease with her then still haunts you, more the loss of it than the presence of it because she got more severe, as if more panicked or cautious the older you grew.

'At first, I thought you levitated, and that was startling enough.' She wiped tears of mirth with her apron. 'But one day, I could not doubt the witness of my own eyes when you willed yourself to location, and there you were in a blink. Can you believe it?'

'Where did I go, Mama?'

'Well. One moment you were in your cot, the next you were sat in front of the home theatre with its holos, flicking pictures of other planets with your mind. You were infatuated with Ekwukwe, Órino-Rin, Wiimb-ó, Pinaa—dear chile! The markets! You always loved markets.'

'Did you always know my magic was growing?'

'I fully grasped your gift when, as a toddler, you quietened a storm. One instant the world outside was rattling, the next all was calm, except for the sound of your magical hum that ran like a stream over pebbles towards a river.'

'Do you have magic also, Mama?'

She looked at you, smiled modestly in a way that told you she'd never disclose to you about her magic. But Baba did. That day he showed you how to fillet a flathead.

'You scale the fish, then slide in like this with the knife, go all the way down. You pull like this, cut the guts on both ends.'

'Do you cut out the bones too?'

'If you're quiet for a minute, chile, maybe I'll show you,' he said.

That is when you asked him about Mama's magic.

'That question doesn't sound like silence,' he said, and put down the filleting knife to contemplate you.

'Does she? Does she have sound magic?' you piped.

'You'll never see her use any of it,' he answered with diplomacy.

'So she does have magic!'

'I've heard whisper of unaccompanied pots that fetched water from the river when she was a young girl.' His voice wore a new timbre, and it sounded like pride. 'I have on occasion suspected her of stirring with her mind brothing fowl on three-hearth stones out in the pergola kitchen, even as she made a bed in the sleeping chambers.' He threw his hands in absolution. 'But it is not my confidence to give, and I haven't seen any of that magic that people think your mother has.'

You considered for a long time how Mama was between worlds, wondered if you were too. You pondered how she inhabited a world of modernity and one of ancestry—how else would you explain a kitchenette of three-hearth stones beneath a louvered-roof pergola? Was that you too? A rough cooking stone on the shiniest arch?

'Why doesn't Mama use her magic, Baba?'

He didn't answer for a long time. And when he did, he said, 'Help me salt and skewer these fresh lizards so we can sun-dry them for rainless times.'

10.

The Guardians took you in after—

There's a flow and movement about the tower of Guardians. It stands tall and lean in angles and edges, ovals and domes. Its sleek walls and gardens present a motion of urgency. Sometimes it hurts your eyes. When first you arrived, you felt dizzy of its sensors and silhouettes, movements and lights. Shifting colour and space switching everywhere. Blues and whites mostly. But there are also silvers, whites and shimmers. Blacks too—the furniture is mostly heartwood, grained, except in the chapel where it's striated blackwood.

The chapel stands at the highest point of the tower, just below the spire. Le'le'pard skin cushions in the nave adorn its tiny pews where nobody but you sits. There's a gilded lectern in the chancel, and at first you had no reckoning what the blackwood bench on the altar was for, until the time arrived for your testing.

Kari'bu said, 'Unless polishing, you're never to touch the bejewelled cups and gilded cloaks in this closet.'

You have no desire to touch them, but it was hard to explain it to Kari'bu because everyone else would have the desire. Your fascination, surprisingly, is with the balcony. Standing aloft you can see the whole world, and it enchants you. It reminds you of duty—not enthralling in itself—but the idea of a whole planet and her peoples trusting you to protect them with together magic, a Hogiiri Hile Halah chant, ash on Hulor Mwe'ra's forehead as he leads the supplication:

'Our Mother watches the wall grow.'
'As anything loved and counselled by Our Mother.'
'We echo the Word to strengthen the wall.'
'As anything loved and counselled by Our Mother.'
'Find the Word. Find the Voice.'
'Khwa'ra. It is acquired.'
'Find the Word. Find the Voice.'
'Ya'yn. It is uttered.'

'Find the Word. Find the Voice.'
'Ra'kwa. It is released.'
'FIND THE WORD. FIND THE VOICE.'
'KHWA'RA. YA'YN. RA'KWA!'

(((

You miss Baba all the time. Baba, who let you sip miracle berry wine, turning Mama apoplectic with chagrin. 'You will ruin her!'

It didn't change the colour, depth or breadth of the chestnut eyes on Baba's kindly face that stayed lit. 'To know the end,' he said, 'one must know the beginning.'

'What end is there in making a drunkard of a chile?'

'Knowledge is the garden we must cultivate,' said Baba.

He never flaunted his magic, even when Mama joked about his gift. Once she said, 'Your father can make a city, let alone a whole house, disappear.'

You remember the day well. You were supping on roasted kalabash and fish steamed moist in banana leaves. Baba's laughter when she said it was a pealing glee, almost childlike, and he clutched his stomach to hold back the laugh that refused to stay in.

He was still tickled as you served a wild mango tart drizzled with fig jam. You made it, and that added the pleasure of serving it. Mama was a superb cook, and showed you how to rest the pastry, how to bake it golden brown until the whole house was sweet with milk and a lingering aroma of butter.

Later you stood together, you and Baba, outside the twin shells of your family mansion. Now you think of it, how the perfect starlight must have spotlighted you between the date palm'palm and the o'livha'vha tree, tall, thin and thriving in your homestead, a tree that bloomed away from its natural habitat of the desert forest. You watched in silence the cascading water falling down the wall of the black stone basin in its tiered rock design. A garden fountain calm and soothing with its crystal-powered lights bought from Órino-Rin.

You contemplated in that silence how Baba's magic was a soft whistle. How yours was the swift run of a flat stream over a stone bed towards the river, and how folk said Mama's was a waterfall.

But she has not used it in many years.

11.

*Ziiiiiiiiiiiiiiiiiiiiiiiiiiiiiiiiiiiiiiiiiiiiiiiiiiiiiiiiiiiiiiiiiiiiiiiiiiiiiiiiiiii
iiiiiiiiiiiiiiiiiiiiiiiiiiiiii
Biiiiiiiiiiiiiiiiiiiiiiiiiiiiiiiiiiiiiiiiiiiiiiiiiiiiiiiiiiiiiiiiiiiiiiiiiiiiiiiiiiiiiiiiiiiiiiiii
iiiiiiiiiiiiiiiiiiiiiiiiiiiiii
tuuuuuuuuuuuuuuuuuuuuuuuuuuuuuuuuuuuuuuuuuuuuuuuuuuuuuuuu
uuuuuuuuuuuuuuuuuuuuu
Ze are ze buzzzzzzz Be are be buzzzzzzzzzzzzzzzzzzzzzzzzz...*

The snakes are sleeping, their wakening replaced by leaves that have entered your head. They crinkle, scratch, chatter and crackle. You can feel the breeze rasping in them, the smell of their odour rancid with dead fish.

12.

Mama understood sound and language, history and philosophy. She sang to you the lost Saúti language the Susu Nunya sought, found and interpreted, taught you about each of the planets and the folktales of its peoples. She told you about the Boāmmariri, the symposium of interplanetary dignitaries that happens every five years right here in the heart of Zezépfeni.

She taught you about Órino-Rin, the planet of mountains and clouds, how its thunder bellowed every which way. About Ekwukwe, the stark planet that echoed like the moans of a ghost, how its beasts like the aze'aze—the giant firefly with the head of a goat—and the impudu-pudu—the lightning bird so big and fiery and smelly—would eat you for sport. About Wiimb-ó and its two spirit moons, Vuiili-ki and Vuiili-ku, that spoke to you if they liked you and you were spiritually attuned.

'There's a place called Savage Mound in Wiimb-ó,' she says.

'Oh?'

'It's a sound island that can be good or bad.'

She refused to explain. Instead, she told you about Pinaa, the land of the tall people who loved machines, how its meteors tumbled in a roar to gobble up young'uns.

Naughty young'uns like you.

You remember the mischief you did on Mama—

You were younger then, just past seven years. It was cruel, what you did. Baba did not smack you to the middle of another year, but he should have. What came upon you to conjure a phantasm, create an illusion that turned a cane toad into a coconut loaf? It was a big toad, the size of two hands and a chin that held its cold slime as you held it back from bounding free. You'd found it behind the cascading waters of the fountain, and clutched at it.

Perhaps it worried you a little, worried Mama too, when she realised the truth of it—did you know how far you meant to go? That was the truth of it: you didn't. Would you have sat still and watched her lift the breadknife? Would you have surveyed how she held down with curled fingers the live toad as if it were bread? Would you have jumped a little, winced or shuddered had she sliced through with the knife's jagged edge, sawing skin and halving the toad through its innards all the way to the board? If she wasn't so shattered, Mama would have smacked you straight into the middle of three days. It was the toad that saved itself, not you, when it croaked out loud and the illusion lifted. Perhaps its croak was a protestation of incarceration between a hand and a cutting board, rather than an outcry in a sentient awareness of the looming terrible death. Whatever the reason, misapprehension slipped and Mama saw the toad in its warts and slime, a white underchin heaving in laboured breathing. She squealed, then, fell silent in a stupor, then found her mind to gaze at you in horror.

Her scream brought your father flying into the kitchen, and he took it all in at a glance. He understood in an instance the malice of your prank. In that bleeding silence that ensued, a centipede propagated its way from the table's underside. Its multi legs shifted its body along the gait of an entrancing wave that, unsuspecting, neared the toad. The saved creature, oblivious of its luck, rolled out a sticky tongue and gobbled the centipede whole, then leapt away into the courtyard.

It was the one time you saw Baba, not mad, disillusioned with you. He gave you a look, and lost his voice. You know that he lost his voice because he opened his mouth, closed it, and turned, wordless, the furthest away from you.

Later you joined him where he sat under the butterfly leaves of a mopane tree, or stood under the tulip tree. You wished, dear Mother, you wished, that he would raise his voice or hand, perhaps grunt at you with harsh words, like: 'Will you never learn?' or 'You were really—?' or 'Was your mother to cook it so you could eat it?'

He said nothing.

Even as you lay your head on his shoulder, felt the softness of his short-sleeved off-white suit. You knew he felt removed from you, from himself, because he didn't lift the long, shapely fingers of his beautiful hands to touch your head. It was as if you were connecting with the suit, not him.

You wanted him to urge you not to remedy the absence you felt inside with magic. Tell you that pranks wouldn't seal the dent in your core, give you borrowed time that helped you forget an uncertain future haunting you with its misgiving for as long as you remembered.

Instead, he just said, 'Now you see.'

What did it mean? You still wonder about this, many years later.

Perhaps, it was Baba's premonition. Perhaps your prank brought a curse into the house, and that was how Baba caught the toad sickness. They called it a toad sickness, although that disease came from no toad. No one knew what caused the wet warts, raw boils bursting on skin. Deformities that leaked the yellowest pus that went grey, and fear entered your eyes. Terror entered Mama's gaze too as Baba's body swelled and burst itself, sweltering with fever.

The summoned uroh-ogi named Mkha'lingalinga arrived sandal-free, breasts flat and free on her chest, her loins wrapped in the black bark. But even she ran out of notions. You watched as she brewed potions, rolled around naked and droned chants, chewed, spat and administered poultices, to no avail. Even her dermalite device that pulsed brightness to illuminate the irregularities of your father's skin was no good. The enhanced glow therapy with nanowater that Mkha'lingalinga sprayed to rejuvenate Baba's skin was as useless as a placebo. He weakly cried when you turned him to administer the therapeutic cold laser and put a cool balm on his pus-engorged lumps. He gurgled like he was dying when you and Mama raised him to change the sheets.

His passing was not easy. Death was a good thing to arrive. It was a kindly thing.

And you never thought you would ever say this.

Now you see, his glassy eyes said before you put out a hand and shut the lids.

You'd like to think he's in Eh'wauizo now, the place of your ancestors. The spirit realm where souls go to rest. But what if he's in a place of unrest, evermore anguished by beasts of unreality?

Spirit of your forebearers rest his soul.

The Guardians took you in after Baba died.

13.

You sleep like a knife. It's cold and sharp, and you dream of a black gleaming under a sun shimmering on hard, frozen water that cuts through time. The sky is black with centuries of regret polished in the brightest eyes glittery as stars.

(((

A new dusk. Life in the tower is repetition. Already it's suppertime, then prayers. Sometimes you wish a fool might find death at the wall. It's a silly thought but you think it. Such an event livens things despite the pelting with stones, the kunkuns and colourful insults hurled at you. Much as you despise it, you also enjoy those mad flights as you blow the horn.

Angry people chasing to hurt you.

When Baba died, way before his casket heaved and sank into hollowed-out ground, Mama stepped into herself and never came out. You had no time to mourn this second death, your mother's inward dying, before your father's peers, the Guardians, came in a shuttle to take you away from all you'd known.

Mama recalled respect and pulled herself together to give the customary greeting. 'Tomorrow belongs to the people.'

'We prepare for it this moment,' answered the one you came to know as Hulor Mwe'ra. He wore the build of a warrior. You remember thinking that, if he trained, he'd be a unit.

Then Mama gave you away.

She didn't hover out in the courtyard waving useless goodbyes as the smooth-nosed, tapered-bodied shuttle lifted for the skies. You remember the radiance, how it powered silent on crystals, Mwe'ra driving it.

It was Hulor Kari'bu, not Mwe'ra, who gave small talk to put you at ease. 'I hear you make apparitions with the ordinary.'

She looked at your hands clenched into a fist on your lap.

'Mama forbade me to use sound magic to do chores,' you said through tight teeth.

'You know you need an eye to thread a needle,' said Kari'bu.

'Yes,' you agreed. 'And fingers too.'

'So you also know you need silence to find the Word.'

'Yes,' you said. 'And belief too.'

She smiled wryly. 'You are young and intelligent, Chant'L. But I fear you're ambitious and way too impulsive.'

'Is that a good thing or a bad thing?'

Kari'bu considered your question, contemplating whether it was curiosity or impudence. Then she laughed. 'You're confident,' she said. 'I like that.' She cast you a curious glance. 'You do know that our work as Guardians is to serve the people, right?'

'Mama said.'

She was quiet for a moment. 'Then why do you act as if you expect people to serve you?'

'I don't know.' You didn't hang your head as tradition required of you, no show of humility or anything like that. 'Because I come from the blood of seekers?'

You don't know why you said it—perhaps it was in relation to your birthing in elite heritage, the Susu Nunya as seekers and keepers of knowledge. But it shifted the mood inside the shuttle.

Hulor Mwe'ra's face grew dark with annoyance at the turn this conversation was taking. 'You're a seeker now?' he barked.

'I didn't say that,' you protested.

'So I am putting words into your mouth?' He glared at you.

'I didn't say that!'

'Seeker of what? Mmhh?'

Even Kari'bu sucked her teeth, her exasperation showing itself. She spat her disdain in a scatter on the floor of the vessel, and you moved your flat-booted feet.

If Kari'bu found this more deeply inciting or amusing, she didn't show it. She found something calming within her and you admired her for it. There was no colour in her voice when she said, 'You lack temperance and the calibre of wisdom that comes with experience and time. There's a reason we're Guardians, not Jurors. Battle is not always about armour.'

She eyed your vest dress that clung to your coning chest, how the skirt like a sarong fell to your flat boots, but spoke nothing of it. The Guardians wore clothes different from what you'd imagined. You'd thought of them floating in goodly religiousness, clad in sack-like attire in the simplicity of a life devoted to prayer. Nothing like Kari'bu's slim-fit coat dress, high-collared and zipped, or Mwe'ra's shiny bodysuit, padded shoulders and a golden breast plate. Thermal-controlled, Kari'bu explained.

You arrived just before dusk and the shuttle landed in an airstrip curved inside a compound that housed the tallest tower you'd ever seen. It stood tall despite its angles and edges, ovals and domes, motion and urgency inside sleek walls. It hosted lustrous gardens that you crossed to meet the outstretched arms of Pita, Jin and Nd'ani.

Pita wore a sleeveless turtleneck jumpsuit, one hand long-gloved to the elbows in what could only be a fashion statement, and Jin, similarly dressed to Mwe'ra in a shiny bodysuit, padded shoulders, only this time with a platinum breast plate. Nd'ani wore a plunge-neck contrast tunic, all mesh in silver and white, and buckled ebony boots.

Kari'bu showed you to your bedchamber where, despite the tower's novelty, you wept.

14.

You're still as uncertain now, as you were then, why the Guardians took you in. A big part of you would like to think their acceptance of you was more for the kindliness in their hearts than for the gift they saw in you. But plenty about them now tells you otherwise. There's not much kindness in them towards each other, even at the dinner table. They quibble like young'uns all the time.

They're at it again as you set out plates, lay out serving dishes and ladles.

Hulor Kari'bu—you think of her as a chameleon, always leaking colour, metaphorically speaking, as you're never sure if you can trust her—is again the one trying to make small talk, like she did in the shuttle that first night the Guardians adopted you. Something about her, especially when she is praying, reminds you distantly of Mama.

'I am working on a new dirge of dreamworlds, a chant that holds dying and mediation,' she says now.

Hulor Mwe'ra lifts his brow, but appears to agree. 'We'll incant it into the Hogiiri Hile Halah chant.' He's the leader but something about him makes you think of ashes. He reminds you of dying woodfire. Maybe once he was a strong one, a leader to unquestioningly follow, just not anymore. You see potential in his stonewashed leadership, what he once was, and are uncertain he's as religious as he presents, much as he loves ritual.

'Incant it into the Hogiiri Hile Halah chant? That is ridiculous,' snaps Hulor Nd'ani in her characteristic aggressive way of disagreeing with everyone. 'Introducing experiment breaks tradition.' Her crooked tooth, the lower canine, is strangely not unpleasant to look at. It shapes her mouth into a pout that perhaps reminds her to be always angry—that's the only way you can explain her temperament to yourself.

'The top of an anthill is not the sky,' slurs Hulor Jin. They are already heady with homebrew, and you know how it scatters their tongue and feet. Jin has a predilection for sweet banana wine the rest of the Guardians do not discourage, but they appear to tolerate them, turn a blind away from their vice. Drinking doesn't weaken Jin's chant. It took time from your arrival to the tower to coach yourself to avoid staring at Jin—the ugliness of them. They have unbalanced sunken eyes, and a receding chin. The disproportion between their nose and lips, eyes and ears, leaves bones jutting out where they shouldn't.

'*I said* we will incant it into the Hogiiri Hile Halah chant,' says Hulor Mwe'ra with careful deliberation. 'The matter is finished.'

Pita makes a sound, says nothing for a moment. Then: 'It is called evolving.' Hulor Pita is an unusual one, especially when he's making magic. You call it tossing haymakers, the weak fists he throws, no strength in the hands. It's as if he's play boxing. The sound magic coming out of his lips in a scraping noise makes you anticipate a ground beast crawling to eat you.

Tonight, you've prepared for them brothed fowl the way Mama taught you: simmered in white pepper, ginger, coriander and saffron. You serve it with pounded cassava softened with the cream of a goat's milk.

Mama insisted that you learn early to use your hands, not that you didn't know how to use them for magic. She forbade you to use sound magic to do chores and lost it if she caught you at it, a broom sweeping by itself, a pot scrubbing itself...'I swear!' she'd snap in that soft voice of hers, and it put chills in you, she didn't have to touch you.

You miss Mama. The softness of her voice even when she scolded you. You linger on her sound, smooth as the feathers of a baby egret. If you could see her just one more time as of old, in a blood-coloured, or whichever-coloured, belly-bottomed onesie that snuggles her voluptuous backside, and flares itself out in flowing sleeves... If you could envision once more for an instant her fondness for rich, earthy hues! She had bum-hugging onesies in all imaginable colours, ranging from blood, ochre, umber, sunny yellow, desert sand to purple-blue rain. She put colour on her nails, on her lips, even her all-weather sandals came in the brightness of yellows, purples, greens, matched with the glowing polish of her small, shapely feet.

You liked to tease her all the time with pranks, not all of them unkind, because she, unlike Baba, reacted. You remember how she went apoplectic when you cast a mirage over her eyes and illusioned a thorned sisal shrub in place of her hand-nurtured flame lilies in the greenhouse. The expression on her face when she looked at the dusty green uglies where her pink blushes, burnt oranges and purple whites should be—

—the weather changed. Or was it you who cast a different season into the horizon?

Mama didn't know how to stay angry long. It took just moments for her to teach you how to make piripiri goat for your father, and serve it hot with malt millet meal. She took pleasure in making sure you mastered the craft of his favourite desserts, as if preparing you for a life without her—that you and he would live a long time, while she died young.

Baba loved durian rice pudding with miracle berry wine, and this is the only dessert you refrain from preparing for the Guardians. You use the rest of your knowledge to feed them. It's an unbalanced rule that exists here. You are the youngest hand, the newest to the tower, which seems to designate you, unvolunteered, to a servant tier.

The pantry is lined with jars of fig jam and papaya marmalade sweetened with cane sugar, all from your hands. It's pregnant with coconut biscuits too, crumbly and crisp, the way Baba liked them.

Now you seat yourself next to Hulor Kari'bu, who is saying, 'The next Ramarire is coming up, the council of jurors.' She hesitates. 'I was thinking—'

'You were thinking what—mmhh?' snaps Hulor Mwe'ra.

'What if we... don't you think... that maybe taking turns might be—' Kari'bu.

'Maybe nothing. Everything stays as it is,' says Mwe'ra.

'But it's always you and—'

'I said. It stays as it is.'

'Ridiculous!' interjects Hulor Nd'ani. 'Must you always represent us?'

Mwe'ra's glance at Nd'ani is cold, then dismissive. 'Please. Pass the salt.'

'A fool will test the waters with bare feet,' says Hulor Jin.

You think of the fool and the bared feet, and cannot be certain if Jin is referring to Mwe'ra, Nd'ani, the situation or anyone in particular.

Hulor Pita makes a sound, says nothing for a moment. Then: 'It is called delegating.'

When Baba on occasion supped with them, you wonder, did he offer them kindness towards each other? How you miss him! His face full of kindness, the deep gaze of his chestnut eyes. You think of touch, and yearn for his beautiful hands—long, shapely fingers. You recollect the distant scent of his pipe on his off-white suit of light texture, short-sleeved, and would give anything for the whiff of it. He wore that suit in service as a specially skilled tradesperson, a Maadiregi, when he went to administer law. The times you didn't think you wanted to grow up and become a Guardian, you'd pondered how it might be to become a Maadiregi.

You think this, as you climb with the Guardians, like you do every dusk after supping, to the chapel. There, right at the top, outside in balcony, just beneath the steeple, you each rub ash on your forehead, and intone behind Hulor Mwe'ra the refrain of the Hogiiri Hile Halah:

'Our Mother watches the wall grow.'
'As anything loved and counselled by Our Mother.'
'We echo the Word to strengthen the wall.'
'As anything loved and counselled by Our Mother.'
'Find the Word. Find the Voice.'
'Khwa'ra. It is acquired.'
'Find the Word. Find the Voice.'
'Ya'yn. It is uttered.'
'Find the Word. Find the Voice.'
'Ra'kwa. It is released.'
'FIND THE WORD. FIND THE VOICE.'
'KHWA'RA. YA'YN. RA'KWA!'

15.

The snakes and leaves are sleeping, no more hissing and crinkling, breezing and ponging.

(((

It's a new dawn, life in the tower repeating itself. You wake, you sweep, you cook, you scrub, you prune. From the green thumb Mama enforced upon you, tending to the holographic gardens of the tower is not especially demanding. Like the crops at home, these ones continue to withstand nature's extremes in the unpredictability of New Inku'lulu's hurricanes and windstorms, heatwaves and droughts.

There are more gifts just out the gate into the courtyard. You collect them. Someone has left a whole bag of owo, the currency of Órino-Rin, and a stash of energy crystals too hard to come by here . You lift a basket of dried fish and deliver it into the pantry. You return to rescue a live cockerel trussed and roasting in the baking sun—there are faster ways of charcoaling it, and mostly with seasoning.

A child steps into your path. 'Tomorrow belongs to the people,' she pipes.

'We prepare for it this moment.' You touch her head the way you've seen Kari'bu do it. 'I grace you with the future,' you add. You nod at the cockerel. 'Is that one yours?' She shakes her head. 'Do you want to pet it?' She smiles and gives you the biggest nod.

You hold the fowl's wings under your arm and let the child pat the crown, even as the bird crows its indignation. The child's mother, big sister or ward is waiting in the distance. Gleeful, the young'un bolts away, turns from away to give you a bigger smile, then runs until she reaches the waiting one. She clutches her face to their knees, as if overcome with emotion, and you understand this.

You connect with youth. You are still young.

You remember how you were an apprentice for one day. How about that? You demonstrated in a single day that came with one sleep what took others many years to master. The entrancement spell is not an easy one, and you were untrained for it.

But you conjured it, first with wind, as Mwe'ra asked, then with water. Kari'bu, Nd'ani, Pita and Jin raised their brows when Mwe'ra demanded that you entrance flames. 'Do it now, mmhh?'

'Your point is?' snapped Nd'ani.

Kari'bu turned her face, as if she could not bear to see you fail. Jin, drunken, staggered away in disgust, unwilling to be part of this madness. Pita made a sound, said nothing for a moment. Then: 'It is called a dirty day.'

Mwe'ra's eyes promised the feat would hurt, and it did. Fire licked your palm as you held it aloft then flung it into a thin space between an invisible wall, the wind still whistling inside, the water still trickling, neither of them diminishing the other. The trinity coexisted unheld, vertical right there in the chancel of the chapel rising high up to the skies.

You noticed how the Guardians looked at each other in wonderment, knew you had conquered the test to become a novice, even as you collapsed with the effort, and was grateful you had another year before the final examination. But Mwe'ra had other plans—

You refused to listen, questioned his judgement. 'Who entraps the beating heart of a fowl?'

'Will you do it?' demanded Hulor Mwe'ra, with a smug face that suggested he thought you were defeated. It was the conceit of him that did it. You staggered with exertion, out of the chapel and all the way out to the courtyard. You looked about, and saw the deep-red hen with spotty whites and greys on its feathers. It pecked alone, away from a black cockerel and its harem of ebony hens. For an instant you doubted, worried you weren't ready.

You needed time! Another whole year to figure out and master this kind of spelling no one had coached you, and now—without the luxury of time—you feared you had failed Baba.

Just then, Baba's silent words: 'Without trying?' He wasn't there but his effect was real.

You find comfort in this thought now, of Baba not far even though he's passed. You don't like to think of death. Isn't dying not a finishing but a crossing? A moving from one consciousness into another?

You step outside, right out of the courtyard and into the world. You're wearing a hood, its cloak covering your breasts that you feel a little embarrassed about, and wonder if, in another life, you were a prince, let alone a boy. This morn you're travelling alone, disobeying yet again the Guardians' ask—that you go nowhere without an errand. You were never one for obeyance, and walking stills your mind from its snakes, bees, leaves, bells and beasts.

You also yearn the world outside. It's a world that's both real and unreal, and this flames your curiosity. Silvered roads, tarred bridges and tunnels, smart laneways, each of them anticipating your tread. There's a vale, an oasis calm with turquoise waters that choke off into the harsh desert country, then spit into smart laneways at your feet, as pulsing silhouettes of shuttles shimmer overhead along the super skyway.

Ziiiiiiiiiiiiiiiiiiiiiiiiiiiiiiiiiiiiiiiiiiiiiiiiiiiiiiiiiiiiiiiiiiiiiiiiiiiiiiiiiiiiiiiiiiiiiiiiiiii iiiiiiiiiiiiiiiiiiiiiiiiiiiiiiiiiiii

Biiiiiiiiiiiiiiiiiiiiiiiiiiiiiiiiiiiiiiiiiiiiiiiiiiiiiiiiiiiiiiiiiiiiiiiiiiiiiiiiiiiiiiiiiiiiiiiiiiiiii iiiiiiiiiiiiiiiiiiiiiiiiiiiiiiiiiiiiiii

tuuuuuuuuuuuuuuuuuuuuuuuuuuuuuuuuuuuuuuuuuuuuuuuuuuuuuuuuuuuu uuuuuuuuuuuuuuuuuuuuuuuuuuu

Ze are ze buzzzzzzz Be are be buzzzzzzzzzzzzzzzzzzzzzzzz...
Chant'L.
The snakes and leaves are no more sleeping.

16.

The snakes are slipping, rattling, tonguing. Slither tracks everywhere inside your head. Hush. Stay quiet.

Sector Z is a strange world with all its random landscapes. Oceans and deserts, beaches and dunes. Morphing climates buttocked between hillocks, vales, canyons and cliffs. As you walk further out, away from the tower, the holographic décor of the city is real as touch. You gaze up at the silhouettes of shuttles overhead, sensors guiding the traffic flow back and forth.

At last you reach the market, and it's just as you remember it from when you visited with Mama. She was always near, never trusting you to behave. How could you misbehave, entranced as you were with the giant shuttles laden with goods and nosing down to deliver their wares? She never understood this.

The shuttles are still wobbling from the sky, lightning in their tails and wings. They arrive from everywhere: Ekwukwe, Órino-Rin, Wiimb-ó, Pinaa... You watch, gript, as traders hoist their temporal stalls and offload carts of freshness and the exotic.

You approach the dress stall, can barely speak in awe. You slip fingers through different fabrics, and the owner of the stall is hawk-eyed about it: 'You break, you pay.'

You can't break fabric, but that's as good as a breaking. There are clingers, thinners, knitters. Shawls, hips, suits, hoodies, buckles, cloaks, meshes. tights, halters, necks, heads, spins, snakes and skins.

'Which one do you want?' the trader asks.

You shake your head and they shoo you off—good for nothing, unless you got dosh that will buy something decent. Or if you have good barter. You have neither dosh nor batter.

The next stall has giant ndege'ndege's eggs arranged in the colours of a sanctuary. There are yellow suns, green palms, silken ants, mud dates and milkweed butterflies. A corner-most egg reminds you of a yucca moth—rainbow-hued from all that pollen, whoring itself from flower to flower. You refrain from touching the egg, or those of the quails, ducks and grouse. You want to use illusion magic, slip one into your pockets, but this trader looks like they know bigger magic, and the Guardians will know from your spell where to find you—that you have abandoned the chores, and the gates of the tower.

Here are fryers—big ones, small ones, flat ones, round ones. You picture a dish in each one of them: a casserole, a stew, a roast, and you wish you did have that dosh or barter with which to trade. Would the Guardians have noticed had you slipped one of the gifts of atonement as market coinage? Perhaps not. But *you* would have noticed, and you have to live with yourself.

You gaze wistfully at the giant pie place just past the jeweller's and the jams and oils. You sample the teas, because it's free and the flavours are all familiar: herbal, turmeric, bark, sunset, malt honey. The merchant sours when he realises you're not aiming to buy any of his wares, and you slip into the sweet stall for its tastings. You point at the hard boiled lollies, fresh breads, cakes, fruits and nuts, and gobble each speared morselet with such lust, one would think you'd been famished half a year.

'Take.' The woman understands. She offers you a marmalade biscuit.

You hungrily mumble a lot of words that can only mean thanks without revealing who you are, and slip off. A muso distracts you from the stall with soaps in coconut creams, lime blossoms, cherry blisses, mango oils and goat milk. He's blind and playing the k'hora'aa. You close your eyes to the sweetest melody of a harp coming and going in a coiling bounce, until someone jostles against you and you hope it's not a pickpocket. It's with great reluctance that you move on to the displays of cloaks, pillows, scarves, sandals, straps and more crystals.

Later, as you ruefully turn away from the smoke and spice wafting from the food stalls, your stomach feels about ready to incite a revolution. The aroma of a horned pig, turn, turn, turning golden brown over a charcoal spit is more than you can take, and you determine it's time. You must make haste back to the tower. The Guardians will notice your absence if you linger too long— Hulor Mwe'ra is a hawk, even when at morning prayer.

It startles you on the way back that a woman recognises you. 'Tomorrow belongs to the people,' she says.

'We prepare for it this moment.'

You tighten the cloak about you, and rush your walk.

17.

The weather has changed all the way back. You'd think you're in a different country. You're accustomed to the mood swings of New Inku'lulu's climate, but an ominous feel haunts the long stretch of hard barren sand under a white, baking sun where just before stood greenery. When you step out of the tower sometimes you never know what you might find, the way this Zezépfeni-lookalike space outpost changes all the time, the temperaments of her vacillating climate: cloud, no cloud, valley, plain, ocean, dune. Will there be small wind, no wind, high wind at speed? Hard white beetles flying at your face are as nonplussed as you are. You remember desert locusts the colour of a dead leaf—crunchy to eat alive. Mama ate them that way, even though you couldn't bear it to watch because all you thought about were oozy innards.

Ants scuttle away fast as if in premonition of a thunderstorm coming.

Ziiiiiiiiiiiiiiiiiiiiiiiiiiiiiiiiiiiiiiiiiiiiiiiiiiiiiiiiiiiiiiiiiiiiiiiiiiiiiiiiiiiiiiiiiiiiiiiiiiiiiiiiiiiiiiiiiiiiiiiii

Biiiiiiiiiiiiiiiiiiiiiiiiiiiiiiiiiiiiiiiiiiiiiiiiiiiiiiiiiiiiiiiiiiiiiiiiiiiiiiiiiiiiiiiiiiiiiiiiiiiiiiiiiiiiiiiiiiiiiiiiiiiiiiiiiii

tuuuuuuuuuuuuuuuuuuuuuuuuuuuuuuuuuuuuuuuuuuuuuuuuuuuuuuuuuuuuuuuuuuuuuuuuuuuuuuuuuuu

Ze are ze buzzzzzzz Be are be buzzzzzzzzzzzzzzzzzzzzzzzzz...

The snakes in your head have begot bees, and these ones have colour: gold and black.

18.

The scene is almost as holographic as if you imagined it.

The incident happens between the ocean and the desert. Right there, beneath the baking heat of two suns scorching your back as down below waves crash on the beach, water cold as a slug but the colour of a jewel.

There she is, how? It's Mau'aa, and she's walking in your direction. It's as if she's come straight from looking for you in the tower of Guardians. She's unorthodoxly dressed in a chain tank top and a silhouette pencil skirt—you can see everything. The outline of her body demands appreciation. You are startled by what you feel, how intensely you feel. It's a new desire that burns your heart, your thighs, wets itself between your legs.

'Tomorrow belongs to the people,' she says, and you know that she knows without doubt it's you. Mau'aa would recognise you anywhere. Her voice is a soft tinkle in your space.

You lower the hood, the game up. 'We prepare for it this moment.'

19.

Your sound magic was always stronger than hers, and it alienated you. No, it wasn't Mau'aa who distanced herself—it was her mother. She came between you and your childhood friend, kindred, blood of your heart. She put a curse on the special something you had with Mau'aa, the most irreplaceable thing, by first casting a side eye that's also an evil eye, then spitting at her feet or close enough to you when you neared. The woman put it in her mind to outcast you from her family, and it worked. Finally, although you didn't hear it from her or Mau'aa about choice, decision or rejection, you knew from the avoidance you perceived that she'd forbidden Mau'aa from spending time with you.

You were angry with Mau'aa, more than her mother, that she complied with the abandonment. You raged against her for not knowing her heart—who didn't? So you did the punishing, not Mau'aa, no. You penalised her mother. First you gave her the seeing of the amphibo, and giant cane toads sprang everywhere she approached seven days straight. Imagine lifting the lid off a pot or a butter crock and a big-eyed toad puffed at your face!

Then you made her see blood a whole day and night. Crimson oozed from her nails, her teeth, her gums stained with blood spraying from her mouth. Blood gushed from her every orifice. It squirted from her eyes, shot from her ears, surely, she thought she was losing her head or fast-tracking without cause to Eh'wauizo, the place of the ancestors.

Baba figured it out. He looked at the poor woman, then at you, and wretchedly said, 'Now you see.'

It was Mama who lost her real head. She put a whole blow to your face. The slap took your cheek, pushed your teeth all the way to the ear on the other side. It should have flown you to the middle of another day, and it stayed a wonder your head didn't snap off the neck and catapult all the way to the market.

'Fix. It. Now,' growled Mama.

And you did. But it didn't put much right. Mau'aa's mother still hated you, and you saw Mau'aa slipping away, further from you each passing day.

20.

Now here she is, Mau'aa, ambushing you from the market. You wonder whether she guessed where you might be and followed you, just to remind you of her rejection, your abandonment. To haunt you yet again with her beauty, and the assurance of never wooing her now that you are—

She's a floodlight of pearls, a boutique of crystals right here and out of reach. How else can you describe her beauty? So close you can touch her but you dare not. You want to put hands on her body, touch her brow where the shock of long braids begins, roped hair cascading down her voluptuous chest. You want to put a hand to each of her breasts in turn, feel the beat of her love-sick heart. You want to slip fingers across her ear, nose, neck, arm, stomach... Would you skip the curly patch, instead glide your touch across her thighs and feel the curve of her knee all the way down to her leg, shin and toes? Would she let you?

As you think these wicked thoughts and wet your tongue, she challenges you with the intensity of her own gaze, and you wonder if she's harbouring similar thoughts of body lingering. But she blinks and dismisses you just as easily as if not, and makes to move on.

'Wait!' You speak with urgency.

Dear Mother, she waits. Mau'aa, beloved of your pounding heart, halts for you.

In that instant, your mind goes rogue and you imagine how you will walk together along the sandy shores, hand-in-hand towards the ocean where you will wade into the waters, lower yourselves into its cool touch, and you will, you will—

How you can remember for a moment her breath sweet as a melon whispering goodly things, doing wicked, wicked things! All at once, you cannot bear it one moment more that you will never know how it feels to grow old together. You are intensely jealous that someone else might look at her like you, think of her like you, touch her like—

You yearn to forget the missing and the lonesomeness, and cannot help but touch her arm lightly.

'Don't.' It shocks you that she pulls away.

'But, but... Why!'

'You have been avoiding me, Chant'L,' she says, 'and I don't like it any more than you.'

'It was the easiest thing, I swear by Our Mother,' you say. 'You know in my heart of hearts that I could never turn my heart from you!'

'You did it to yourself. You made a choice.'

'Choice is reckless, don't you see?'

She looks at you fully, the night in her eyes calling, calling. 'Is this how you will flirt with me, endlessly across year to year?' It's not acceptance or rejection. There's almost a plea in her voice.

You're a head and a half taller than her. Now you will kiss her, it's the only natural thing. She leans, featherweight, into the arms you put around her. It's as if she has swooned, and will fall if you let go. She shuts her eyes as your mouth caresses her eyelids, first one, then the other, her nose. She opens her lips and you swallow her mouth with all of yours. It's your first kiss and the sweetest. She is mango and cantaloupe and miracle berry and wild sugar cane. You're kissing, kissing, a forever kiss.

Ziiiiiiiiiiiiiiiiiiiiiiiiiiiiiiiiiiiiiiiiiiiiiiiiiiiiiiiiiiiiiiiiiiiiiiiiiiiiiiiiiiiiiiiiiiiiiiiii iiiiiiiiiiiiiiiiiiiiiiiiiiiiiiiiiiii

Biiiiiiiiiiiiiiiiiiiiiiiiiiiiiiiiiiiiiiiiiiiiiiiiiiiiiiiiiiiiiiiiiiiiiiiiiiiiiiiiiiiiiiiiiiiiiiiiiiiii iiiiiiiiiiiiiiiiiiiiiiiiiiiiiiiiiiiiiiiii

tuuuuuuuuuuuuuuuuuuuuuuuuuuuuuuuuuuuuuuuuuuuuuuuuuuuuuuuuu uuuuuuuuuuuuuuuuuuuuuuuuu

Ze are ze buzzzzzzz Be are be buzzzzzzzzzzzzzzzzzzzzzzzzzz...

The snakes and leaves and bees and bells and beasts rouse in your head with a growl, and are flying and crawling, shuffling, vibrating inside. They're hissing and crinkling, humming and tinkling, howling and howling. They say you shouldn't be here. Not alone with this girl. She's an addiction. A deadly addiction. And it's calling out your magic that's tumbling out in shapes of snakes, leaves, bees, bells, beasts, together with a monstrosity of sound that falls from your mouth.

Mau'aa is screaming and screaming, her fingers curling against your chest, pushing from the creatures flowing out of you, but they won't let you ease your clasp on her, won't ease your hungry lips from her fear. And there's a fog, or smoke or a chant swirling around your head, groaning, looping, arching, whirling, and you're forgetting where you are, who you are.

The crushing blackness.

Help!

21.

You come to. It takes a small while to remember who you are, where you are. Where is Mau'aa? You glance around in panic. There she is on the ground, lying in stillness next to you.

'Oh! No, no, nonono!'

You get a little closer, grab her and shake her. 'Mau'aa!' She's quiet in your arms. 'This is no time for play!' You shake her. She's cold and quiet. Her grey skin is harsh to witness. You utter a cry.

Now you see what you've done. See what you've done! What you and the snakes, leaves, bees, bells and beasts have done. You roll as far as you can from Mau'aa's lifeless form, glance at it in horror and the most complete disgust at yourself.

Ziiiiiiiiiiiiiiiiiiiiiiiiiiiiiiiiiiiiiiiiiiiiiiiiiiiiiiiiiiiiiiiiiiiiiiiiiiiiiiiiiiiiiiiiiiii iiiiiiiiiiiiiiiiiiiiiiiiiiiiiiiiiiiiiii

Biiiiiiiiiiiiiiiiiiiiiiiiiiiiiiiiiiiiiiiiiiiiiiiiiiiiiiiiiiiiiiiiiiiiiiiiiiiiiiiiiiiiiiiiiiii iiiiiiiiiiiiiiiiiiiiiiiiiiiiiiiiiiiiiiiii

tuuuuuuuuuuuuuuuuuuuuuuuuuuuuuuuuuuuuuuuuuuuuuuuuuuuuuuuuu uuuuuuuuuuuuuuuuuuuuuuuuuu

Ze are ze buzzzzzzz Be are be buzzzzzzzzzzzzzzzzzzzzzzzzz...

Must get away from here, get away. Go!

You use your sound magic, think yourself someplace like Mama said you did as a bub, take yourself any place away from here, and find yourself in the intimacy of your bedchambers inside the tower. You snap the door shut with unuttered sound magic, you think it and it happens, then cry out your grief.

You contemplate deeply what happened, and don't have answers why.

The rest happens so fast.

In hindsight, you could have summoned Mau'aa's body to the Hogiiri Hile Halah, shaped your mouth and slipped in fingers, taken a deep breath and sounded the whistle of summon.

And it would have been win-win. After the blowed horn, folk would have understood that one of their own had breached the place of reverence, sullied it with their touch. And, none the wiser, they would have come along in ones, twos, brought their gifts of atonement. Cowrie shells, millet brew in gourds, coin, crystals or cockerel. They would have laid them with reverence out in the courtyard for you to collect. Them, you could have fooled.

But the Guardians—promptly summoned by your magic to the precise scene of the crime before anyone could contaminate it out there in open country—are not fools. They whisked the dead girl's body away, examined it even though it's a task that doesn't need much talent, let alone the skill of a guardian. Anyone with sound magic can trace the signature of enchantment on a deceased person directly to its source, if not to almost within range.

A rhythmic clapping in a rise and fall accompanied by a chant-filled harmony tells you the Guardians are coming, and they will judge you, mete out punishment. You panic in that instant about what they might do to you. What if they make you run around Sector Z wearing nothing but the skin you were born with, horning and declaring your malevolence, telling everyone who'll listen how you killed one of their own? They'd pelt you with eggs, stones, insults all the way. You fear to think what Mau'aa's mother will do to you.

It could get worse. The Guardians might banish you from the tower, return you in shame to Mama, still mourning. Mama who stepped into herself and died, and died. Now you will kill her again with the shame of it all.

They sweep in a hurricane into your room, and all except Jin—who has lost true kindred, poetic Mau'aa who looked nothing like them, no bones jutting where they shouldn't—grab you. Jin is necking a bottle of sweet banana brew without drowning in drunkenness.

Everything you feared is not what happens.

'Will you expel me?' you cry out frightfully, as they drag you all the way up to the chapel.

'Expulsion?' snarls Hulor Mwe'ra. 'That's too easy and unlearning, don't you think, mmhh?'

You squeal your fear, cower on the altar as justice falls swift in the song of Our Mother.

'Joramjoramjora,' echoes Mwe'ra, repeating the words in an ancient hum. 'The Word echoes outward, and we who utter the Word—'

'Are witness to its power,' chant Kari'bu, Nd'ani and Pita in unison.

Jin mutters something, and is all hyper, bouncing off walls, chanting as if possessed in that scratching noise of a ground beast crawling to gobble you.

The snakes in your head are slithering tongues out, their scales rattling, unasleep in your universe. You're resisting their magic with your own, mentally battling to set yourself free from the Guardians' unity without you, their together magic that is stronger than alone magic.

Hulor Kari'bu sways in the pleasant melody of her chant. Her mouth is open to the right width and shape to flow the music of the creation myth that must now uncreate you.

'Her tears flow vast oceans, bind to the dust of the Word,' she hums.

'Forming soils and stones. Joramjoramjora,' echoes Mwe'ra, in a strange acceptance of Kari'bu's lead.

And your snakes, leaves, bees, bells and beasts are bellowing out of your mouth, then screaming and screaming. It takes the sound magic of four Guardians to bind you. The agony of being bound hits you worse than the venom of a tarantula.

Something is pressing against your chest, sucking out your breath like you did Mau'aa's. Now you're cold and quiet, feeling grey and dead all over.

22.

Chant'L. Your name is Chant'L. You try to remember this, who you are, because every part of you claims you're a monster. The Guardians think so too, or they wouldn't have trussed you like this on an altar as they further ponder your fate. That's more than a kick in the loin when someone is down.

You feel grief, just not in the mourning kind of way. Your angst manifests itself in the deepest and most clutching form of the missing, the lonesomeness, a core part of you taken. You felt the missing when Baba... when Mama... You felt the missing way before them, and now it's here in all its gloating when... Oh, Mau'aa, sweet Mau'aa! You feel the missing, and much rage. Such fury at Mau'aa who has gotten herself killed in a stupid, stupid way.

You didn't mean to do it. You didn't ask the magic to harm her. You have failed her as a Zezépfeni kindred, as a guardian, as a lover. Even love could not protect her. You'd bring her back if you could, wouldn't you?

Yet here you are imprisoned in sound magic, weakened and lying on the blackwood bench altar. Trussed with invisible strings like you once did the fowl when the Guardians put you to the test. There it was, feet up and still, and you were meant to bring it back.

(((

It was your final examination of entrapment. Hulor Mwe'ra stood by the gilded lectern in the chancel, nod, nod, nodding, as you walked into the chapel with your pick of fowl from the courtyard. He nodded, watching how you restrained the fowl's wings with a glance. You nuzzled it up to your neck and gently pushed it down on the blackwood bench.

The bird lay feet up, supine under your spell, heartless, because you had magicked out its heart that pounded by itself inside an invisible wall for seven days. That was what entrapment did. It put something alive inside a wall and, once mastered, you could work it on the Nga'phandileh, the malevolent beings of unreality. You could work together magic with the rest of the Guardians to make sure the Nga'phandileh stayed entrapped inside the Hogiiri Hile Halah.

What astonished both you and the Guardians is that you didn't need to keep chanting the prayer of Our Mother to maintain the entrapment spell. The fowl's heart still beat as you went about your chores, sweeping, scrubbing, stir-frying, weeding. Then on the seventh day you blinked from a distance and, without touching, released the heart from the invisible wall and installed it back into the fowl. The bird startled and crowed indignation. It made sure you understood its disgust in the wet squeeze of green and white poop on the altar, before it scattered and flew in a rage out of the window and all the way down to the courtyard.

Later, in the courtyard, you stood and watched the fowl. As if it had forgotten, or was still lured by some spell, it walked in your direction unbidden, pecking unabashed. You wondered what it had felt, where it'd gone, when it lay feet up on the striated bench under your sound magic. It let you pet it, even squatted under your touch. You pressed hands around its wings, without magic, and it gave a low rumbly sound. You cradled it to your chest, rubbed its belly and spoke softly to it, even as you wrung its neck.

You defeathered it in a pot of scalding water, broiled it and served it to Guardians with a garnish of crisped leaves and purple flowers, and a grating of carrots and cabbage drenched in vinegar in egg-shaped bowls each. Cabbage was so overrated, you recollect thinking. The Guardians munched flesh, spat bones. Only Hulor Kari'bu pounced on the truth of the dish—you could tell from how she eyed you with sorrow, pity or both.

'Wood touched by fire will set ablaze,' she spoke to her plate.

(((

Now you remember those words, trussed up as you are with invisible string like the fowl atop the striated altar bench. Will the Guardians munch you, spit your bones? Or perhaps Kari'bu will save you.

They have encircled you in a chalked ring around the altar, and wrath at your treatment is overcoming your dread of what's coming.

Ziiiiiiiiiiiiiiiiiiiiiiiiiiiiiiiiiiiiiiiiiiiiiiiiiiiiiiiiiiiiiiiiiiiiiiiiiiiiiiiiiiiiiiiiiiiiiiiiiiiiii iiiiiiiiiiiiiiiiiiiiiiiiiiiiiiiiiiiii

Biiiiiiiiiiiiiiiiiiiiiiiiiiiiiiiiiiiiiiiiiiiiiiiiiiiiiiiiiiiiiiiiiiiiiiiiiiiiiiiiii iiiiiiiiiiiiiiiiiiiiiiiiiiiiiiiiiiiii

tuuuuuuuuuuuuuuuuuuuuuuuuuuuuuuuuuuuuuuuuuuuuuuuuuuuuu uuuuuuuuuuuuuuuuuuuuuuuuu

Ze are ze buzzzzzzz Be are be buzzzzzzzzzzzzzzzzzzzzzzzz...

'You have a mouth that makes the wrong sound,' Hulor Mwe'ra says. Blue and red fire blazes in his eyes. 'A fragment inside you is uttering deadliness, and do you know what we do with a rotten fruit, mmhh? We put first hands on it and pluck it out.'

'What Hulor Mwe'ra is saying—' Kari'bu tries to explain.

'You must suffer the Silence,' barks Nd'ani.

'To know silence is to learn,' slurs Jin.

Pita is wordless for a moment. Then: 'You must learn the right way to wield the Word.'

'And the way to do it is in the Silence of fulfilment,' explains Kari'bu.

But even she hesitates when Mwe'ra says, 'Bring the tools.'

'Perhaps the punishment is too much?' Kari'bu says quietly.

'Our Mother created, never destroyed,' says Mwe'ra. 'The chile must learn.'

'But Our Mother also loved and admired,' says Kari'bu. 'We can teach in other ways.'

'Our Mother made whole, never crumbs,' says Mwe'ra. 'What do you think Our Mother would suggest we do with this chile, mmhh? She must be clipped before she decays us all.'

'Sand does not hold water,' Jin's boozy words.

Pita is silent for a moment. Then: 'Sand remembers every drop.'

'Could Our Mother love even more?' asks Hulor Kari'bu.

It delays but does not save you from your fate.

23.

That first night at the tower, the day your mother gave you away, you were so terribly homesick. You consoled yourself that Mwe'ra, Kari'bu, Nd'ani, Pita and Jin took you in, accepted you into the tower, because they understood your magic.

As you curled on the long, thin bed that was soft, but not as soft as your memory of Mama, as you missed the palm trees and coconut trees of your twin-shell home, it was Kari'bu who came to you.

'It never goes,' she said. 'The missing.'

'What can I do?' you asked, hopeful she might have an answer. 'To numb it a bit?'

'What you can do is remember duty,' she said. 'Understand and recollect why you're here. Why we're all here.'

'I don't know why we're here,' you said childishly.

'We're here because we protect. That is what we Guardians do. Do you know much about the Nga'phandileh?'

You shook your head.

'Do you know *a little* about the Nga'phandileh?'

You shook your head again. She smiled and sat on your bed.

'Let me tell you about the Nga'phandileh.'

And she did. She was a gifted storyteller, perhaps not better than Mama, but it made you consider if Kari'bu had Raevaagi blood in her heritage—a gift of the bards. She painted with such vividness canvases of broken worlds that fell to ash and rubble when the Nga'phandileh, beings of unreality, let loose. Sicknesses worse than Baba's putrid sores leaking yellow, yellow pus until it was grey and smelled like the buttocks of a dead impudu-pudu—this time whole faces melting and tiny babies dying in the worst pandemic to strike Zezépfeni, and the rest of the planets: Ekwukwe, Órino-Rin, Wiimb-ó, Pinaa. As if that was all. You now understood the damning effects of a global madness that possessed people and made whole villages attack each other with axes and hammers in a forever war, until an emergency Ramarire met, an urgent symposium of Jurors, and it was reasoned the

Nga'phandileh had to be contained and Zezépfeni was best placed to do it with a veiled wall.

'We maintain the reality border from creatures of unreality, those that hide in the cracks of creation—we must keep them at bay,' said Hulor Kari'bu. 'To do so takes a new kind of knowledge, and humility. First there were only Jurors. And now also Guardians in Sector Z. We chose to put down armour and embrace the illumination of the Word.'

'Oh?'

'But we are still soldiers. Every day is battle. There's no reasoning with Nga'phandileh. Some say only the aura of a taq'qerara can subdue the beasts of unreality,' Kari'bu mused.

'A takirra?'

'Special born. There's the story of a taq'qerara named Ruk who lived—hear this, not in Zezépfeni.'

'No?'

'Ruk lived in Órino-Rin. He was unable to hear sounds but could feel sound aura. Maybe we wouldn't need the wall if we had more taq'qerara in New Inku'lulu, mmhhh?'

'I want to be a taq'qerara,' you said.

'Why?'

'So I can subdue the Nga'phandileh.'

'It is not a gift that comes with wanting,' said Kari'bu kindly, but with firmness to make it clear. 'And, actually, I told a half truth. Legend suggests you need more than the aura to command the Nga'phandileh.'

'Oh?'

'You need a splinter, special magic, from Our Mother.'

'Like the folklore of a rib to create another?'

'Like the folklore of a rib,' she agreed.

'I want to get it,' you spoke earnestly. 'A splinter.'

And Kari'bu laughed at your eagerness for the impossible.

You felt trust with her and found yourself opening up to her, telling her about your longing for the scent and texture of your bed at home. You told her about the mopane tree back home, how sometimes you climbed it the hard way, frog-climbed with hands and feet all the way up and dangled on the topmost branches, then slid down for the thrill of it, rather than think yourself up and down the tree. You told her about Mama's voice, soft as the feathers of an egret, even as she scolded you using more words than Baba ever did.

You told her that Mama home-schooled you. That she was a descendant of an intermarriage between the Susu Nunya, the keepers of sound history, and the Raevaagi. You refrained from asking Kari'bu outright if she too had the blood of bards, tellers of history. Instead you said, 'It's a good thing celibacy was not necessary for the Susu Nunya, otherwise I would not have been born.'

'That's right,' said Kari'bu in that ponderous way of hers.

(((

Ziiiiiiiiiiiiiiiiiiiiiiiiiiiiiiiiiiiiiiiiiiiiiiiiiiiiiiiiiiiiiiiiiiiiiiiiiiiiiiiiiiiiiiiiiiiiiiiiiiiiiii iiiiiiiiiiiiiiiiiiiiiiiiiiiiiiiiiiiii

Biiiiiiiiiiiiiiiiiiiiiiiiiiiiiiiiiiiiiiiiiiiiiiiiiiiiiiiiiiiiiiiiiiiiiiiiiiiiiiiiiiiiiiiiiiiiiiiiiiiiiii iiiiiiiiiiiiiiiiiiiiiiiiiiiiiiiiiiiiiiii

Tuuuuuuuuuuuuuuuuuuuuuuuuuuuuuuuuuuuuuuuuuuuuuuuuuuuuuuuuuuu uuuuuuuuuuuuuuuuuuuuuuuuuuuu

Ze are ze buzzzzzzz Be are be buzzzzzzz Te are te buzzzzzzzzzzzzzzzzzzzzzzzzzz...

The Silence is not a silence.

The chapel door opens. It's Kari'bu. The reacher, the connector. Of all the Guardians, she's the one always doing the visiting. This time she comes to see you, not in your bedchambers as she did on your first night when she told you about the planes of existence, how the Nga'phandileh lurk in a dark place behind a wall. She attends to you in the imprisonment on an altar.

Her eyes say there's a boundary line and you have crossed it: What shall we do with you?

She'd forgive you if it were her choice. But it isn't.

'I told you about that hot head and impulsiveness of yours,' she says quietly.

You can't say anything, and she sighs.

'I also told you that what we do is protect,' she says. 'We are Guardians. That is what we do. We keep the people of Zezépfeni safe.'

She looks at you sadly. 'Where did it go wrong, and it felt right to bring harm to people?'

You want to explain, but what words will make her understand that it was not a thing you'd planned to do. Who goes out thinking: This day I will break my celibacy. Kiss my heart's yearning, steal every breath out of her so no one else can have her? Well, there are some who might, not you. It was the snakes. The leaves. The bees, bells and beasts.

But Kari'bu is not looking for answers. All she has are questions: 'Does a hen destroy its own eggs?'

24.

The day Baba died there was a feast like it was a wedding. The djembe drummer from Ekwukwe flew his hands and feet, and people bopped everywhere.

You took forbidden cassava brew, necked it like Jin does now, and took a swig to wash down the roasted chicken feet, gizzard curry—they let girls eat it, only for this celebration of a passing, even though it was a special delicacy for the men. You gobbled fermented yams and peanut stew, washed that down also with the brew. And you woke up to the headache it gave you. The migraine of a sun-baked, unslept warrior who had just won battle at a terrible cost.

(((

Is this how the Guardians see it—a battle won? At what cost?

'It will last only a moment, but it will be a most terrible moment,' Kari'bu speaks quietly to you from your altar prison, but it does not shift the sternness from her gaze. 'You'll finally comprehend what unreality feels like.'

25.

They clasp you with hands strong as steel. They hold you down and use a brace to widen your jaws—it is Hulor Mwe'ra who inserts it. 'This is what happens, mmhh?' The clamping, each pinch of the pincers that rip a groove off your tongue is an agony you will carry to your grave.

A song of gnawing pain rivets from your toes to the crown of your head. The first stanza pulls out urine, to your deepest shame. By the third groove, yet another rip in your tongue, you're ready to pass out for agony, but wretchedly don't.

Have some emotional awareness, 'cos this badly hurts, you want to say. How can we move forward with this? But you're bound in a spell of paralysis. You can only beseech with your eyes. What happened was wrong, let's start anew.

You're conversing with boulders.

26.

There's a coffin. Why is there a coffin? You might be in trouble here, you think wildly, perhaps for the first time truly understanding your plight. No. No. Nonononono. Then you calm yourself.

It's for Mau'aa. They will give her a decent sending off to Eh'wauizo, the place where souls go to rest. But why can't you see her body? Where is your beloved Mau'aa? No one has prepared her for burial. No. They will not put her in a casket. They will char her body with sound magic, and it will explode and vanish in a great, big smoke that will free her soul from malevolence so she can reach Eh'wauizo.

You look at the coffin. Nonononono. It has bail handles screwed to the outer wall of its side, enough for five Guardians, even a drunken one, to hoist it. The elegance of it, solid timber and gleaming fittings—if you didn't know it was destined for you, you'd say the casket was pretty. There's nothing pretty about what the Guardians intend for you.

Did someone donate the coffin to the Guardians, or do they have a reserve, lots of deceased beauties, to punish wayward ones like you? Because the ones that died at the wall did not go into a coffin.

No one answers your unspoken questions.

They are too busy putting you in the coffin. Wait, no. The curve-shaped lid closes. Hulor Mwe'ra is the turnkey who locks you in, but you can see everything through the polished wood. It's as if you have the sight, a magical seeing. Too little colour, too much silence.

Your soundless shrieks rake the air. The moral of the story is—

The wondering, the thinking: What if they never let you out? That's what makes it worse. They are hoisting you. No. No. Nonononono.

Now you're out in the courtyard. Animal instincts stray your gaze from your daze. You cast eyes from fabrics to faces, limbs... punitive hands clutching the wrong sort of severity. What you need is kindness. Dirty-handed is still kindness alive with reaching.

Help me!

They're wearing sombre robes. Funereal ones in a pale grey, hooded with long sleeves. You can't see their faces. The Guardians are of similar stature. This observation astonishes, as you'd never considered before what likenesses the Guardians held. Without colour, voice or appearance, you can still tell them apart. You know exactly which one is Mwe'ra. Kari'bu. Nd'ani. Pita. Jin.

Mwe'ra—the arrogance in his shoulders, the robe tracing the harsh angles of his frame. Kari'bu—leaning, as if wanting to reach you, how can she help you? Nd'ani—aloof, 'Far is best,' her figure is saying. Pita—weak. You could push them over from the grave. Jin—swaying with inebriation, sunken face inside the hood. Mwe'ra. Kari'bu. Nd'ani. Pita. Jin. A unison of digging with shovels. Some magic needs exertion to make it stronger, bind you firmer.

'It will last only a moment.' Kari'bu's repeated word, from somewhere in the distance, bears less sternness. She is suggesting a temporal void. Until the grooves of your tongue heal. Until you relearn your chant. Will they take you out of the tomb then?

What she doesn't understand is the permanent nature of the hate their chastisement manifests inside you. Baba is gone. Mama is gone. Mau'aa is gone. You have nothing but loathing. Hatred that grows as a shovelful of soil thuds the lid. The ground is closing. They will never let you out.

No. No. Nonononono!

27.

That is how they took your magic.

Unreality is dark and deadly and it stirs inside you. Unreality is a grimness full of omens that spit against you. Unreality is solitary and wrath, and they tower above you in shadow, sometimes grey, sometimes cerise, and what you feel is buried.

(((

You remember it over and over. How they took your grooves, buried you with Mothersound.

'Your voice is a good one for magic,' Hulor Mwe'ra had said, menace in his voice as he made ash of your torn tongue with flames in a crucible. 'But you must use it for GOOD.'

'You must take this as a gaining,' said Hulor Kari'bu. 'Not a losing.'

It was as if she'd forgotten that she was a Guardian. Why didn't she protect you? That first night at the tower when she visited your lonesomeness—the night you talked and talked about your mother, about planes of existence, about Nga'phandileh that lurk in a dark place behind the wall—did it mean nothing?

(((

The beasts beneath your skin are hungry. They turn you inwards in the chaos of your fog, and you see time zones, fractal shadows sliding from a singleness searching for itself. You seep and scab, muted in the unmapped terrain of multiworlds cast upon you.

You're erased. Your life is in groans, loops, arches and whorls. You're nothing but a fleeting presence looking in, looking out. Shadows are easier, outlines without detail. Shadows can bear it better than you—you're worse than a shadow. You have detail yet don't exist. You're yearning for something wrapped in fog, smoke or chant, something that leaves a trace so you don't forget who you are.

28.

You're hungry, so hungry. You think of wet, casseroled sausages on a black clay plate. Something you know keeps you awake and jittery. Something that says, without sound magic: *Chant'L, you are nothing.*

In the deepest misery, your fullest moroseness, you remember the folklore of the sonic fruit, lying there dormant, yet ripe, and all it was capable of. All it needed was inner magic, finding its own sound, to become the sonic flower it truly was.

(((

Somewhere in your disquiet, Mama is calling, calling. You seek her, and there you are, there she is. You're a chile, and you're sat under the mopane tree, praying together at dusk in the rain.

'Our Mother,' chimes Mama.

'Our Mother was all,' you pipe back.

'She the only reality—'

'—in a boundless sea of unreality.'

'There was no other to behold Her,' she says.

'Her light the only light.'

'No other—'

'—to receive Her light.'

'No other—'

'—to reflect Her light,' you say.

Mama takes your hand. 'It's bedtime now, chile. Let's get back inside and take these damp clothes away.'

'But I want to stay here.'

'That's why there is tomorrow.'

(((

Mama's voice gives you strength. Unreality is dark, deadly and it will not take you. Unreality is a grimness full of omens but light is shimmering through a hole. Unreality is solitary and wrath, and you're not alone.

You feel it, the sound magic.

You have fists to break a casket. Claws to dig yourself out. You're no more buried.

This new you grows new feet, wings, fins. Sound magic frees you from your body, and you're a Le'le'pard, tail switching, black, gold and tan rosettes on your fur. You're a bird, a fish, you're more than you know. You're running, soaring, swimming, demons on your back. You dissolve in the air, and the sky, and the water. The world puts the weather out for you, restating it's no glitter future. The tempest is a shell, coned and targeting. Its unwet murmurs in your ears. It tastes of salt, or perhaps that's you, sweating as unseen water rises, thunder hollering at the world, and at you.

You're in motion again. A fierce wind travels you, gives you many options pulling you this way, that, as it takes part in your disarray and the excruciating rage throbbing inside your raw mouth. You collapse in a shadow storm, and a dust devil nearly takes you. *It's your past*, a bird or a trap sings. *Too much going on.* Your body screams back at it, until the bird or trap is hushed. You travel incognito, ears ringing with fate. A spectre strikes a steady blue flame in your face. But nothing moves, not even you, until the presence is gone.

You shake loose, slip back into the shadows. You try to find choice, how to reinvent yourself, convert opportunities and begin to make sense. Somewhere in your fever dream, you're free, free, and the Guardians are looking at your fleeing backside—your mama certainly gave you one, and there's a lot of it for them to see!

You're invincible. Nothing can harm you. What magic can beat this? You're running, swimming, flying, free, free, unfree! The Guardians, that's what. Together magic is no match for alone magic. The Guardians have found you, and it's no dream. Their sound magic is thwarting your escape. You yank, you heave. They pull, they tug.

They are out of reach, too far from Zezépfeni to haul you back. But they're too near, close enough to entrap you inside an orb.

You're falling, falling. Your body is as it was, no longer invincible. No wings will soar you to safety. Water will not catch you, no fins will move back and forth to thrust you along whichever destiny.

Clouds end your fall into a quietus too close to the bone and it wires your anxiety, stokes your yearnings, many, all of them for home.

29.

You're imprisoned, looking down through a giant orb. The world down below—it looks like Wiimb-ó. You know this place from Mama's stories. It's Savage Mound, the sound island of Wiimb-ó. It is animal shit. They are animal shit. Mwe'ra. Kari'bu. Nd'ani. Pita. Jin. They're the Guardians who made you. The Guardians who destroyed you.

This is the compromise of your alone magic and the together magic of the Guardians.

Sound magic has exiled you here, right in the heart of the soundless cloud.

The cloud is an open grave. You're closed in the orb.

You peer through the orb in a transmigration of self. You must reinvent yourself, no one else will. Nothing will notice you. *Chant'L, you are nothing.*

You hold yourself close, because no one else will.

30.

The Silence is a question you never hear but you know it's there. It's a dark room behind curtains your terror has sewn shut. It keeps you awake and, unlike Zezépfeni, nights here are long, fissured with cold. You yearn for home, not this unbelonging. Kari'bu warned you—

what unreality feels like. But this is not unreality. It pains you too much not to be real.

You curl into your orb and think of how your home where Baba lived, Baba died, is resilient to the weather's viciousness. You muse about granite walls, the pergola. How Mama loves to cook on a three-hearth fire. You think it over and over, singing yourself to solace with these words, over and over.

> *Mama loves to cook*
> *on a three-hearth fire.*
> *Three-hearth fire*
> *three-hearth stones.*
> *Mama loves to cook.*

You dream of the waterfall cascading down the tiered rock fountain back home. The soothe of its waters as you let them run over your fingers. Shiny lights crystal-powered everywhere. You think of the greenhouse. Ebony trays sprouting peas, radishes, beans, tomatoes, sunflowers.

> *Mama loves to cook*
> *on a three-hearth fire.*

You think of her light lilies. Red tongues inside purple flowers glowing in the short dark.

> *Three-heart fire*
> *three-hearth stones.*

You're imprisoned in an orb full of silence—you must make music in your head.

Ze are ze Zi Ze are ze Zi Ze are ze Zi Be are be Bin Be are be Bin Be are be Bin Te are te Tu Te are te Tu Te are te Tu

The bees are humming.

How have they entered your head here too? A whole hive of them, messy in their odour. Wings beating in slow motion between your ears. They are flying, hovering, foraging. Building an invisible nest right here in your brain, stitching it with blended chatter. Bzzzzzzzzzzz. It climbs to the highest pitch, until you can make out words in trilogies of sound:

> *Ze are ze Zi*
> *Ze are ze Zi*
> *Ze are ze Zi*
> *Be are be Bin*
> *Be are be Bin*
> *Be are be Bin*
> *Te are te Tu*
> *Te are te Tu*
> *Te are te Tu*

The wall is here. The Hogiiri Hile Halah. The invisible wall that trembles, pulses, buzzes, gorges and destroys. It's calling out to your magic.

31.

It's animal shit. They are animal shit. Shitshitshitshitshit, all of them. Mwe'ra. Kari'bu. Nd'ani. Pita. Jin. They are the Guardians who made you. The Guardians who destroyed you. Together they are the Guardians. You were the Guardians.

The Silence is not a silence.

Ze are ze Zi
   Ze are ze Zi
      Ze are ze Zi
         Be are be Bin
           Be are be Bin
           Be are be Bin
              Te are te Tu
               Te are te Tu
              Te are te Tu

The fog is a yawn. You adjust yourself from aberrant wondering, and peer through your gaoling orb. The horizon disappears and, for a moment, you feel terror. But the crystal is clear downwards, and now you see it: a whole new world with its huts and chalets, markets and rivers, all intimate through a seeing bowl.

You long for companionship.

The longing is a press on your chest that crescendos until it bursts in your core like thunderclaps again, again and again. You peer again through the orb. The world below is a grid—its lanterns a glaring yellow, some screaming white inside the meticulous order of Wiimb-ó. Why must *you* be exiled, and not them?

32.

It's a forever exile. How can anything last this long?

You dream of ground. You look up from your gloominess on Savage Mound, the place of your banishment in the butthole of nowhere. Fog floats you on the sky inside the giant crystalline orb. Sometimes, you feel you're it, Chant'L. You feel you're the fog.

You peer downward.

A hut door snaps open, then you see no more. The morning is a muted blue.

So you hum a silent song that goes round and round, and it reaches—

—an open-aired market.

Its colours remind you of Mama. Mangoes, pumpkins, sweet yams, red cabbages, bananas all vibrant in blood, ochre, umber, burnt yellow and desert sand. Cheerful yellows, lively purples, optimistic greens.

The market is overflowing with baskets and baskets of goods, urchins squatting inside palm-leafed stalls by their wares. A drummer is turning the rope on a djembe drum, tuning it, and you wait, expectant.

You pray it is a spirit drum, but the view blanks out before he can play it.

33.

You dream of ground. You startle from unsettled sleep, peer downward through the orb. Light shimmers under the crack of the hut door that snaps open. A mud-skinned child tumbles out with a basket. The djembe muso is turning the rope to tune his drum. His hands and feet are flying. You can't hear the drumming, it's too distant.

You're trapped in a sound island.

34.

You dream of the ground. You startle from unsettled sleep. You miss Zezépfeni despite its changing seasons. You miss how nights are short and not very dark. Here, meteor strikes are less but nights are long and so very dark. Wiimb-ó at dusk is too black. It lasts a lifetime.

You peer downwards through the orb. Light shimmers under the crack of the hut door that snaps open. The mud-skinned, curly-haired child, perhaps five years, tumbles out with an empty basket. It's a yellow straw basket. She races barefoot towards the market.

The djembe muso is turning the rope to tune his drum. His hands and feet are flying.

The Silence is not a silence. You can hear the drumming. They are spirit drums bellowing into your sound island. *Doombadoo, doombadoo, doombadoodoodoombadoo.*

The drums have awakened the bells now pealing in your head.

Ze are ze Zi	*Be are be Bin*	*Te are te Tu*
Ze are ze Zi	*Be are be Bin*	*Te are te Tu*
Ze are ze Zi	*Be are be Bin*	*Te are te Tu*

Doombadoo, doombadoo, doombadoodoodoombadoo.

The spirit drums are telling you a story.

(((

'Tell me about the wedding!'

'Your Baba was quite a get,' says Mama to your little self. 'His smile was this big.'

She stretches her lips. 'You know how he took my hand with his fine, fine touch? Like this.'

You clasp her back with your little fingers.

'Did he take you straight to the wedding?'

'He took me first—'

'Where?'

'Patience, chile. Your Baba took me all the way to the best Zéhemgwile, sons and daughters of the guild of tailors.'

'Oh?'

'He took me there for our nuptial fitting.'

'Oh!' You eye her onesie that knows she has the hips to wear it. It's belly-bottomed and flare-sleeved like the rest, this one the colour of violent rain. 'Did the Zéhemgwile make you a fine dress?'

'They made a silver cloak, collared to my cheeks, and it hugged my chest in royal plaids.'

'Ohhhh!'

'It stole flames from my necklace of t'lazanini and t'sasavotite beads, and sparkled my bracelet until it shone black and gold—'

'Ohhhh!'

'You should have seen the shimmer! It's entered people's eyes, burned and stayed there.'

'And Baba?' You can't picture him in anything but his off-white suit, short-sleeved.

'Your Baba, he wore a holographic suit, it was three-piece—a blazer, a vest and pants, all slim fit. His cufflinks came from the d'hiamomo and rhorhodolite mines in Ekwukwe.'

'Ohhhh!'

'I found him this breast kerchief that matched the flame lilies everywhere in the nuptial citadel, which was a place you hired, shimmering in reds, gingers and yellows. There were hyacinths, proteas, honeysuckle and orange blossoms too. Whiffs of wildness and baby-fresh everywhere.'

'Did you drink?' you ask, even though you know Mama is not a drinker.

'I sipped a little to ease the nervousness. It was the best cassava mashed by feet—'

'By feet!'

'—to turn it into wine fermented in a drum for three years.'

'Three years! Tell me about the food!'

'Everything was there. Wild fowl. Boer liver. A nine-tiered marula cake the shape of a palace. And this muso came from Ekwukwe, played the k'hora'aa, the luhte'te, hands flying on the djembe drum. Doombadoo, doombadoo, doombadoodoodoombadoo.'

The spirit drums are telling you a story.

35.

There she is, coming back—the mud-skinned, curly-haired child, five years, heaving from the market with her yellow straw basket. Her face is furrowed. The basket is increasingly heavy for her, but she will not allow it to defeat her. She reminds you of yourself.

You peer closer.

There are crabs inside the basket. They are trying to escape, climbing on each other's heads with white claws to crawl out. There are pink crabs and dark greys. The greys are more aggressive. They are tufted ghost crabs, hair on the tips of their eyes. The ones that nearly fall out—

She whacks them on the head, straight back into the basket.

36.

First thoughts are honest. They speak from your core. Never from soft verges or jagged margins. But sometimes, like this day, they tell in the tongue of uneven language taking time to shape itself.

Meaning is unclear inside all this swirling of sound. Hisses and hums catapulting every which way. Rustling and murmuring inside your head. In between the sky and the grid, high up away from the living down yonder, there's nothing.

Only you, a pointless blot from it all.

(((

Memory sharpens your starvation for living.

You remember the hot springs you visited back home in Green District, a bunch of several families finding solace together in winter. You were too big to cuddle against Baba's chest from his lap as you did when you were little. This time you waded in naked, you and Mama—Baba and the menfolk on the other side where they couldn't see you.

You stepped into healing water that smelled of farts and spoiling eggs. Sizzling water all turquoise spat from hot rocks. Blue steam full of minerals helped your skin breathe. Despite the water's smell, its touch on your skin was the most soothing hug sweltering from ebony stones surrounded by soft, wispy trees.

You wanted to see Mau'aa, and you did see her. Despite the bracelet you gave her in secret away from her mother's distrust and disdain, the two of you couldn't sit close to each other. You watched how she fidgeted, unable to sit still. How she stole glances at you, even with the straight line of her mother's lips. You remember how the sun caught Mau'aa's chin when she turned. You'd wondered then how it would feel to run a finger on her wet skin. How it would feel to lick her skin in rain.

But you stayed away for her sake, and Mama's, who scowled at you. You thought your mother's displeasure was something to do with a girl liking a girl. She didn't say it, and you did consider asking why she appeared to take a side when it came to the matter of you and Mau'aa.

Afterwards, you wanted to take a shower, wash it all off, more the lonesomeness than the farts and eggs in the water's foam. But Mama said no. 'Don't wash the water's kiss.'

(((

Ze are ze Zi	*Be are be Bin*	*Te are te Tu*
Ze are ze Zi	*Be are be Bin*	*Te are te Tu*
Ze are ze Zi	*Be are be Bin*	*Te are te Tu*

The Silence is not a silence.

Down below trees tremble. They remind you of having failed, because you're up here and alone, an exile. You want to tumble down to the child, to the market. You touch clouds in your mind, try to remember reality, but a soundless voice tells you to forget.

You don't forget everything. How can you forget when all you have is hover and regret?

You peer down the orb.

Light shimmers under the crack of the hut door that stays shut. But you can see through its walls as if they were invisible. The mud-skinned, curly-haired child is tipping the basket. Pink crabs and the tufted ghost ones tumble into a large pot of scalding-hot water. You imagine their hiss, rasp, click. Sound climbing to high squeals.

The child adds vinegar, takes five breaths. Scoops a crab out with a ladle. It's boiled alive, now a deep red.

Declawed.

(((

You feel declawed. Without sound magic, you're nothing.

37.

The Silence is not a silence. The beasts in your head speak in trebles of trebles.

> *Ze are ze Zi*
>   *Ze are ze Zi*
>   *Ze are ze Zi*
>   *Be are be Bin*
>   *Be are be Bin*
>   *Be are be Bin*
>   *Te are te Tu*
>   *Te are te Tu*
>   *Te are te Tu*

Bells, all these bells! Pealing, vibrating, dancing, tinkling, clanging, chiming, smashing, squeaking, piping, wailing, dinging.

Ding, ding, ding!

A giant eye is watching. It's a side eye, not a glad eye. A turning tide and you know it's coming from the other side of the universe. It's the eye of a creature wearing skins in a ripple of others it has already eaten, and they are many in all sorts: pockmarked, branded, freckled or tattooed—

> each of which you will
> never judge or save
> a door snaps open
> there's a child.
> Repeat.

38.

The Silence is not a silence. The beasts in your head speak in trebles.
   Ze are ze Zi
   Be are be Bin
   Te are te Tu
The bells have summoned the snakes have summoned the leaves
have summoned the bees, all active at night, the long, long night of
Wiimb-ó.

you
peer
downward
a mud-
skinned
curly-
haired child
perhaps
five years
tumbles
out with
an
empty
basket
a
yellow
basket
she
races
barefoot
to the
market
it's
happening
on
repeat

39.

One day after the rains when the suns Zuúv'ah and Juah-āju shone, you tugged Mau'aa's hand and went with her to the forest between a canyon and the red desert.

You picked a clump of fresh reishi mushrooms, sun-kissed from the wetness of before. They were shaped like the ears of an ancient woman, and fruit-scented. You slipped two medium-sized split gill mushrooms onto her palm, slipped them just to touch her skin.

It was Mau'aa who found the young kingtubers and their hint of ocean.

'Smell them,' she giggled.

You put them to the nose, but they smelled like nothing, only you didn't tell Mau'aa. You also didn't tell her that sometimes they're bland to eat.

Instead, you said, 'Let me show you the puffers.'

You hunted a long time, on the move here, there, scratching like fowls. You rummaged the ground and fondled the barks of trees. You found only milk caps and inky caps until, finally, wild puffers. They were large and fleshed like steaks with the sweetest smell and taste of nuts.

You took care and gently pulled Mau'aa from plucking the death caps.

'They take you in a cruel way,' you told her. 'The way you did, even Eh'wauizo can wait.'

You split your harvest, not equally because you gave Mau'aa way more than half. She carried them home in the skirt of her dress. Mama saw what you brought, and was chuffed!

'You're a chile of Our Mother!' she cried.

She leapt in her glee and flew about the pergola, tossing up black mushroom soup for Baba. It was another of his favourites. She infused the rest into black mushroom pilau with thyme, cloves and roasted tomatoes. Other mushrooms she stir-fried with crushed ginger and smoked paprika inside the char-bottomed pot. It was a decent harvest. She had enough to save for a slow-braised mushroom sauce with sea salt and golden peanuts. You wanted her to roast what was left to eat with baked sweet bananas, but she didn't this time.

(((

Like all stories, there's a beginning, there's an end. The gut, the belly of it—that's where the most trust is. That's where you find a seed, a leaf, a flower, a weed. Or a scar in the shape of an omen.

Your scar is healing. Your tongue will never grow back its grooves, but it will know new sound. You yearn for what you've been, for where you've been, but what you feel is absence. Each absence merges into another, naming itself, interchanging itself, again, again in an unloving space of tight, cold lips that amplify your need. You're ashes and ice in the pit of your stomach, sleep in staggers full of weeds. The darkest nights arch and stretch, mutter through dawn about home.

Life is destruction—no distinction between left, right, boundary, borderless. Sound is magic. Rhyme. Repeat. Difference. Resonance. Reverberance. Somewhere inside is reverence. It's animal shit. They are animal shit. Mwe'ra. Kari'bu. Nd'ani. Pita. Jin.

Your heart is a wall, a maze to nowhere good. No labyrinths of light, just shards of brokenness. A boulder enters your stomach and stays there, edges scraping you all the way inside.

Unseen. Misplaced. Silenced in a land with no seasons, guarded inside an orb.

A deep craving in your core claws at you, tells you with much knowing that you must end before you begin. Is your leaving the arrival of your redemption? Must you die to resurrect? In the deepest gloom, no ash on your forehead, you cry out your newest distortion of the Hogiiri Hile Halah chant:

Our Mother loves and counsels me.
I am the Word. I am the Voice.
Khwa'ra. I acquire it.
I am the Word. I am the Voice.
Ya'yn. I utter it.
I am the Word. I am the Voice.
Ra'kwa. I release it.
I am the Word. I am the Voice.
How is my Word not good?
Khwa'ra. Ya'yn. Ra'kwa!

40.

First.

What you feel is wrath, then lonesomeness. They come in order.

In the core of your deepest solitariness, you call for a companion and two devils gyrate into the orb. They crouch just so, and you're at face level. They leer or study you, and decide you're safe.

Each offers you a hand, invites you to your feet, and you dance together in a trinity of being, wrath and lonesomeness. You twirl, and twirl, abandon yourself to a turbulent swirl, shimming and flirting, embracing space and time, as your bodies twirl, twirl, a trinity of blur and you're tingling with promise and letting go. Your fog slowly dissipates with each boppity-twirl. You untangle from the embrace of your companions, Solitary and Wrath, who say in unison, *Listen.* And you hear the whisper clear as dawn.

ZiBinTu

ZiBinTu

ZiBinTu

You gaze at Solitary—her intense lonesomeness manifesting itself in a towering greyness that puts a tombstone in your stomach. *Listen,* she says mournfully.

You turn to Wrath—her intense fury, a morphing cerise that forms, deforms and rushes blood to your head. *Listen,* she growls.

And you cannot deny it, this turning point in an old song, a new arrangement of fantasies itching to make a mark that's all about them, and they're inside your head.

ZiBinTu

ZiBinTu

ZiBinTu

41.

Fog heaves the last of itself off, and you feel calm, blissful for a moment.

It's in this oblivion that, unexpectedly, you notice the twins. How long have they been there? You know what they are, Mama taught you. They are Vuiili-ki and Vuiili-ku, the twin spirit moons of Wiimbó. They are not personified, as they sometimes appear to folk. At first they are faint white glows in the sky, but the more you stare at them, the more colour they pitch at you—a luminescent milkiness, then fluorescence that's gold-tinted with splashes of auburn, lilac and fuchsia. Their aurora shimmers, engorging the ebony horizon until it's kaleidoscopic.

You sit, transfixed, in the embrace of sublime beauty that's also a resurrection.

Solitary and Wrath, your new companions, are curled alongside you, each resting a head on your shoulders. Solitary is the gloomiest she can be, Wrath trembling in her ire. What's this now? You squint at the firmament, at licks of crimson with blue tails shooting across. A thrill races through you, imparts a puzzle and a truth you never thought to notice in an eon, and it skips in your head all the way to—

—New Inku'lulu. You're here, you're there. And then someone is here, right there, in a onesie the colour of indigo rain. She's winking in and out of the horizon, her words breaking through the sound island. *Magic is inborn, never truly taken.*

Mama? Your words fall out, new, disembodied on your tongue. Are they true words, or simply thoughts?

Dawn will always break, she says.

Are you really here, Mama?

You remember every drop of the water you carry. This is the truth. So remember it, and find strength. Stand up for yourself.

And then she's gone, yet she isn't. Her voice, soft as the feathers of a baby egret, is still there. *The power is in you and the spirit world is calling. You see, yet you unsee. Must someone else chew food already in your mouth?*

Mama!

Who do you expect to question for you why Vuiili-ki and Vuiili-ku are here now?

I don't understand!

Perceive the realm of your ancestors. Snatch back what is yours.

The echo of her voice touches you everywhere. *It has always been yours, yours, yours. See, see, see. The spirit-light is fullest now, now, now.*

42.

ZiBinTu

ZiBinTu

ZiBinTu

It happens on repeat. The hut door snaps open. The mud-skinned, curly-haired child is back from the market. She's tipping the basket. Pink crabs, tufted ghost crabs, tumbling into a scald of water. Hissing, rasping, clicking, squealing. She adds vinegar, stirs the pot three, five times as crabs boil alive. A deep-red legless one ready for eating in a ladle.

You snatch yourself from the world below, observed through an orb, and contemplate your mother's words, how true! Magic is inborn, never truly lost or taken. The Guardians could never take it away from you.

It makes sense. What you have is an opportunity to reinvent yourself. You rise to your feet and try to summon the kind of magic that pulses loudest in spirit-light. Your sound is nothing like a swift stream over smooth pebbles towards a river. What comes out is harsh. Broken. The river is hot-headed and rushing to throw itself across a crag in a monstrous waterfall. It distorts your Hogiiri Hile Halah chant but, no matter the sound, it's there all the same:

Our Mother loves and counsels me.
I am the Word. I am the Voice.
Khwa'ra. I acquire it.
I am the Word. I am the Voice.
Ya'yn. I utter it.
I am the Word. I am the Voice.
Ra'kwa. I release it.
I am the Word. I am the Voice.
My Word is GOOD.
KHWA'RA.
YA'YN.

RA'KWA!

The fulsomeness of your sound magic throws you against the orb, and it shatters. You are no longer a prisoner. You're free, free, free. Alive! You need not die to find redemption!

Solitary and Wrath tumble howling into the firmament that vanishes them back to wherever it was they sprang from. The spirit moons Vuiili-ki and Vuiili-ku are swollen at their fullest. Night is bright as dawn, pulsing, pulsing, then ebbing.

You look around. No more Solitary and Wrath for companionship, but you're not alone. The snakes, the leaves, the bees, the bells, the beasts are falling from your breath, and personifying, transmuting, amalgamating. And the smell! It's musty, a nasty odour of rotten eggs and faeces. You gag, there's no getting used to that terrible whiff emanating from a morphogenesis that's beyond your comprehension.

Now they are one, an amorphous beast rising to full height, and identifying itself. 'Zibin'tu.' It's the menace of a beast you have born, too many hypnotising heads. It towers over you, each of its heads swaying. 'Zibin'tu.' It's bigger than a t'embo'oo, the largest tusked animal that roams the forests of Ekwukwe, and insists on its name. 'Zibin'tu.'

You are looking at many eyes like glows, and suddenly burst into laughter. It's a mirthless sound that falls from your lips, your hand on your stomach trying to hold it back in, like Baba. There are tears on your face and you're laughing, crying, laughing, crying.

'Zibin'tu!' bellows the beast. 'Master!'

This is not good. Apprehension cuts short your mirth, cry—does this beast think it's your master? You blink, no longer chortling in manic, befuddling emotion. Indeed, what you feel now is horror. '*What* are you?' you cry out.

'Zibin'tu. Master! Ze are ze Zi. Be are be Bin. Te are te Tu. Zibin'tu.'

'What *lunacy* is this!'

'Master! Ze are ze Nga'phandileh. Be are be Nga'phandileh. Te are te Nga'phandileh.'

You understand what's happened. It's a trinity of Nga'phandileh, Zi, Bin and Tu. Is it the same one that has haunted you since you were a child. How is this possible? Somehow you have enabled it to escape the Hogiiri Hile Halah all that way in Zezépfeni. The Nga'phandileh,

Zi, Bin, Tu... The trinity has found you all the way here in a singularity of beast that has named itself Zibin'tu!

'Master.'

And you were wrong about one thing. No.

The transfigured Nga'phandileh is here to observe your commands. Nonononono. With a gasp of horror, you understand what you are. Nonononono!

'*What* do you want?' you whisper in fright.

43.

'Master!'

'Get. Away. From. Me!'

Is the beast a beast when it crawls from your shell to avoid conversation, blinking nothing just its mouth like a fish on its way to dying and using up its last breath to say, Ohm. Ohm. Shhhhhh. Shhhhhh. Is the beast a beast when it walks, bent-backed and curious, and you cannot forbid it from looking for a better life on a dusk to remember? Is the beast a beast when it no longer prowls in your head, but is unwary in the sound of your restored magic that collects the smashed orb, shapes it into a lidded jar you will use to entrap the beast?

But Zibin'tu tears away from you and falls with a terrible howl from the cloud, spearing in the blackest fog to the world below and you realise too late where it's headed.

Look what you've done. Just *look*, what you've *done*.

You stare aghast below.

44.

Questions drive you mad, and you remember Kari'bu's words, how the Nga'phandileh can steal logic, make you obsess and linger in unreasonable dread. What have *you* done?

You scratch your head in trepidation, try to step into the boots of wisdom. What would Baba have done in this position? He would have said in little words, few but prudent words: 'Tell me about the Nga'phandileh.'

What do you know about them? Nothing! Nothing except what Kari'bu said. A tremor sweeps through you as you recollect the bad, bad things Kari'bu spoke of. Broken worlds swirling with fire from the earth's core. Sicknesses worse than Baba's and making babies' faces fall. A pandemic of madness that steals memory and ancestry and folk kill each other like mindless tikolokolo, spirit gremlins.

You don't understand why Zibin'tu called you master, because you're not a taq'qerara. And, by no means, do you possess a legendary 'splinter' from Our Mother, special magic to command the Nga'phandileh, even though you said you wanted one. Kari'bu made it very clear that to be a taq'qerara is not a gift you ask for. It's inborn.

So what does Zibin'tu want?

You find yourself in the habit of stepping into footwear, and now try and put yourself in hir shoes. What would you want if you were a being of unreality? You consider this for a moment.

Perhaps you'd want to take form, snatch back your own physicality from the inexistence of entrapment spells that held you captive for eons inside a wall. And that's exactly what Zibin'tu has done, claimed hir own reality. Made hirself at last seen.

Zie called you master, and this gives you hope. Perhaps you might contain Zibin'tu, coax hir back into the wall. Your magic that released hir is the same sound magic that will entrap hir again. You may not be a taq'qerara but you know now exactly what you are.

45.

You're a Nga'phandileh whisperer.

You feel a certain pride in your kinship with the anomalous trinity Zi, Bin and Tu that has named itself in a singularity of Zibin'tu. You thrill for a moment in the potential deadliness of the Nga'phandileh trinity that now calls you master, in the potential deadliness of you against the Guardians and all who have wronged you.

But Mama's aura shimmers in your inner eye, reminding you of duty, of responsibility that comes with sound magic harnessed by spirit-light. And Baba, Baba. His voice, a distant echo. *Now. You. See. See. See.*

Then you panic!

You remember again what you've just done!

You've unleashed the Nga'phandileh to the humans.

You're still on the orb-free cloud and looking below, which is a bit stupid. Together with the sound magic you summoned with your rehabilitated tongue, the spirit-light from Vuiili-ki and Vuiili-ku accomplished what you sought it to do. Restored you to bigger, stronger. The once imprisoning orb is now a jar in your hands. Now you command it. If once you walked the clouds with bleak feet, it's past tense now.

Suddenly, you feel a terrible need to go. Not to descend to the huts of Wiimb-ó, or return back home to Zezépfeni. What you want is the barest nature, you want to find a latrine and relieve yourself. It's the topmost priority because otherwise urine rain will be falling on people's heads! Sound magic bound you, now nature calls.

You tuck the jar that was once an orb into your vest, and think yourself aground.

46.

You're surprised it's almost dusk. The view here in reality is far different from what you saw in a daze from high up on a sound island through an orb. The wilderness you witness now is certainly more than the impression of Wiimb-ó you gained from height, which is a bit unsatisfactory, given how much you've longed for people and civilisation.

A beast is prowling in your head, and it's growling, roaring.

You're standing outside the hut you've seen over and over, but its garden is overgrown with special t'embo'oo grass that must have come from Ekwukwe and there's something about the idea of snakes you're not comfortable about. It's bad enough they coexisted in your head—you're in no rush to go stepping on one. But you must go, and the need is now, and a bush is here.

You squat into a brush that's all green and fat, small-leafed. Its stem is a succulent red. Your piddle squirts in a forever rush that goes on and on. Finally emptied, you shake yourself in a crouch, then pat yourself dry with a leaf.

You rise and look about the boma. There are no farm animals as you might expect outside a hut. No hens and roosters pecking aimlessly, and this is not a good thing. Because you are so hungry, you would have bitten one raw and swallowed it whole, gobbled everything, even the feathers and feet. You're so hungry—when did you last sup? You're ready to eat a thrice-dead impudu-pudu, the lightning bird, slurp up its seeping innards and lick your fingers one by one after, if not eat them as well.

You eye with hunger the succulent brush shivering wet with your piddle.

No! You reprimand yourself at the idiocy of the thought.

Light shimmers under the crack of the hut door that snaps open. The mud-skinned, curly-haired child tumbles out with her yellow straw basket. You blend with the bush, and the t'embo'oo grass is scratchy, itchy like the milk of a sisal plant.

It is with gladness that you realise you're not stalking the child, that you're not hungry enough to want to eat her. You watch as she races barefoot towards the market, and then you approach the hut. You push the door open and slip into the sparse area that's all a single living, cooking, sleeping area.

Sure, it's humble inside, frugal more like it. An insect's web glistens along tiny parts of the round wall, mud-bricked, and you contemplate if it's an edible critter. You're riveted by the floor—rich with the odour of polished dung, as if freshly surfaced. An oil lamp aground flickers orange flame and you pick it up to look around, studying the sole furniture of a three-legged stool, a blackwood armchair draped with bad-smelling animal skin—perhaps some giant lizard that may have produced the dung. Here's a section that must be the kitchen with its clay pot on three cold hearth stones.

The growling, roaring in your head is coming and going as if from a distance.

Shadows follow as you peer about, poke around the hut, not that there are many secret rooms to peer at. You touch and test for bounce a legless nest that must be the bed, and it's made of grass (not t'embo'oo) and a soft blanket of egret feathers—you'd know them anywhere. Astoundingly, the scant bed does have a bit of spring in it.

The hut is swept clean, even though there's an old smell of dung and a whiff of ocean about it. Nothing tells you who the child lives with. There's not much colour, except for what's in the clay pot. No plates or bowls, forks or spoons. Guilty, yet unable to help yourself, you lift the ladle and scoop freshly-boiled crab. The meat is salty and sweet, soft and not chewy.

The growling, roaring in your head is loud, louder. Still hungry, you glance wistfully at the now empty pot. It looks scrubbed, emptied of all its crabs, that's how ravenous you were. You hope the child is returning soon, of course you will not eat her! Such a foolish thought—

The child!

It shames you that only now your starvation is satiated does it strike you how much time has passed since the child left, and she has not yet returned. You walk out of the hut and peer in the direction of the market, you think that's the right way, as you saw it from the orb and things are different down here.

You want to witness her homecoming, watch her heaving from the market with her yellow straw basket laden with new crabs. You want to see her furrowed face, the basket getting increasingly heavy. What would you do? Maybe approach her, do your best not to startle her, offer to help with the basket if she'll let you. She doesn't look the kind to allow much to defeat her. Matter of fact she reminds you of yourself.

As if only now attuned to the sound, you realise the growling, the deep roar is not in your head. It's in the distance.

A high-pitched scream shatters the air. You hear a howl, the sound of a woman wailing loudest, and the tumult is coming from the direction of the market.

The child!

Another abysmal screech pierces the dusk. And you can smell the air now, infused with a musty, nasty odour of rotten eggs and faeces.

Dear Mother. Oh no!

You think yourself to the market and face in horror the destruction.

47.

You're facing a wiped-out market—all this the work of a fraction, barely a miniscule, of the entirety of Nga'phandileh. Just three malevolent Zi, Bin, Tu, weakened with sound magic, yet unified in a singularity. Now look! A man is crawling from the edges of a crushed stall. He is reaching with a hand, reaching for—

What?

You watch in a state of shock as wounded, stupefied merchants unify to rescue one of their own. They pile on, shouting and crying, heaving and huffing, and they manage to move away timber and stone levelled to the ground over the ill-fated man. Eventually they pull him out, but it's only a torso of him, the rest gone.

Zibin'tu swoops in new attack. Hir deepest black fog is tailed with a bolt of lightning and a horrific bellow. Screams rise and fall in the tempest's devastation, a fierce wind hungry to ravage an already torn market, blood and debris everywhere.

You whip out the jar that was once your imprisoning orb, and face off with Zibin'tu, who is crouched to your height and looking for a fight.

You grit your teeth. 'Get. Back. Here. Now.'

'Master.' There's no respect or obeyance in hir voice. The heads are swaying, the eyes ruby. It's more like rebellion, perhaps a questioning of your power—what, really, can you do?

You wear Mama's stern voice, point to the jar and snap. 'I said. Come. Here. Now.'

Zibin'tu rushes at you.

The attack sprays you to your feet. Suddenly you're smothered in black fog that clouts, jaws, punctures and grapples you. As you wrangle with the malevolent trinity now a singularity, you recollect the colourful insults of the people of New Inku'lulu back home. Their outrage, their disdain at the ritual of atonement.

It feels like a giant snake is squeezing the life out of you. You throw your sound magic with your fist and splay your fingers, at the same time hurling out your insult.

'You thrice-shat, regurgitate of a constipated p'hobawawa!'

Who cares the insult makes no sense?

'You outcast of people excrement!'

Hanging by a yarn for your life, you chuckle a little about that insult. Not only is zie an outcast—human excrement won't have hir anywhere near! Oblivious, Zibin'tu is tearing at you, breathing out what can only be flames because something is singeing your skin and everywhere burns.

'Stop. It. Now! I am very close to having enough!'

As if Zibin'tu will listen.

You look beseechingly at the cowering traders encircling you as if it were a wrestling match for coin. Some look like they've put a bet on it. You spit out a tooth, wrestle with the fog that howls at you in ferocious thunder, lightning and gale. It mauls and tears, swipes at you with teeth, stings and venom.

Upset, desperate and scared, you cry out the Hogiiri Hile Halah chant:

I am the Word. I am the Voice.

Khwa'ra. I acquire it.

I am the Word. I am the Voice.

Ya'yn. I utter it.

I am the Word. I am the Voice.

Ra'kwa. I release it.

Sound magic gobbles Zibin'tu and hir ear-piercing screech inside the jar, but zie is humping and resisting the lid you're trying to get back on. You're battle-wounded and don't need anyone to tell you that you're swollen-eyed, puff-cheeked, raked in all shapes and sizes across your skin. Your vest dress that once clung to your coning chest and flowed at the bottom like a sarong to your flat boots is fully ragged and you're as good as naked.

Furious at how this is turning, a complete debacle, you incant again:

I am the Word. I am the Voice.

My Word is GOOD.

KHWA'RA.

YA'YN.

RA'KWA!

The crowd of surviving merchants nursing all manner of brokenness eyes is cheering from a distance. Applaud shares around, but folk fall away in terror as you raise the victorious hand clutching the magicked jar capped tight with the Nga'phandileh inside it.

Applause gets bigger, but the sense of victory is short-lived. The jar is making a warbling sound. It's shaking and stretching, distorting, reforming, and you glance at it with severe worry. You don't know how long Zibin'tu—excitable from all that wrecking and bloodshed—will hold inside the jar. The crowd is not waiting to find out. Even the wounded ones are running very fast away from you and the cursed jar.

You're alone, but now you have another concern. You look about and use sound magic to scatter the ruins, limbs, stones and wood, searching for the nameless child you're yet to make acquaintance with.

'Little one!'

You fling yet another obstacle and peek hopefully underneath the debris. 'Little one!' There are tears in your voice. 'Please. Young'un!'

What in your past would you change for the sight of the child pulling herself from the wreckage, belly crawling herself to safety? Just then, the ground rocks and bulges. With a terrible bellow, it begins to sink itself into a fissure the size of a beast's belly. Those in the crowd who were not fast enough, especially the injured, are clawing, slipping into the ground's maw, teeth forming to ground them into its core. You think yourself to the edge of the mauled earth. With a wet gurgle, a hot black porridge forms in its belly—on it the charred bones of the dead it has claimed.

You look at the forever crater where a market once stood, and are unable to fathom the maliciousness of its hunger that ate men, women, children. 'Little one! Please. Young'un.'

Rageless, impersonal, but still. Just as deadly. First Mau'aa. Now all these people. Chant'L.

You

    Did

       This.

48.

The jar is forming, deforming, pulsing with the black fog of mischievous Zibin'tu. You eye in panic how the fog inside is twisting and tugging, now curling in foetal position in the jar, and you fear you've bitten more than you can chew.

You may be a Nga'phandileh whisperer, but you're yet to learnt how to train it, contain it. Now the fog in the jar is splitting itself into three distinct shapes ominously wafting against the glass. And the snakes and bees and leaves and bells and beasts are back in your head, louder than you remember them.

Ze are ze Zi Ze are ze Zi Ze are ze Zi Be are be Bin Be are be Bin Be are be Bin Te are te Tu Te are te Tu Te are te Tu.

You never thought it possible but you miss Mwe'ra, Kari'bu, Nd'ani, Pita and Jin—them all. You miss the Guardians who made you. The Guardians who destroyed you. Or did they? They are your together people. Perhaps you unmade yourself. But now you're new, you're different, and you want to learn. Mwe'ra can teach you! He's an old Guardian, the woodfire of his lifetime dying, but there's much teaching in him still. How is it that you miss him now, he who disliked you so? He was never religious but loved ritual. You remember the care with which he applied ash to his face to echo in an ancient hum: 'Joramjoramjora.'

You want to see Kari'bu, who you can trust, and yet cannot. She's a chameleon leaking colour, never strong on one side. You want to listen to the pleasant melody of her chant that reminds you of Mama.

Nd'ani, for all her anger, talking hard all the time like a street urchin, has good sound magic that comes out in a grunt, furious as it is. You need it to contain the Nga'phandileh, and need all the help you can get. You cannot whisper the Nga'phandileh alone. And maybe you need Pita, tossing haymakers with his magic that comes out like a sick donkey's cough. Drunken Jin too, the water-hole guardian, unbalanced yet potent on sweet banana wine.

The jar bucks and hops by itself by your side where you're seated at the topmost lips of a dissolved market, a world that has gobbled itself and now floats the bones of dead people on its surface. You look morosely at a snake in the fog, a fat, writhing thing covered in ochre and black scales, moving despite its bigness inside the constriction of the jar. You're not as petrified of snakes as you were before. But the presence of this one is still disturbing.

Ze are ze Zi Ze are ze Zi Ze are ze Zi Be are be Bin Be are be Bin Be are be Bin Te are te Tu Te are te Tu Te are te Tu.

You think gloomily of the child with her basket, the calamity you've caused, as big, even worse than what happened to Mau'aa. The snake is writhing in slither tracks inside your head, hissing and rubbing its scales. Blinkless eyes stare back at you. And there's a smell you can't dispel. An odour of putrid cucumbers.

You need the Guardians now more than ever.

Of your own volition, you must walk yourself into the slow teeth of a short night with its space and colour—blues and whites.

49.

Ziiiiiiiiiiiiiiiiiiiiiiiiiiiiiiiiiiiiiiiiiiiiiiiiiiiiiiiiiiiiiiiiiiiiiiiiiiiiiiiiiiiiiiiiiiiiiii iiiiiiiiiiiiiiiiiiiiiiiiiiiiiii
Biiiiiiiiiiiiiiiiiiiiiiiiiiiiiiiiiiiiiiiiiiiiiiiiiiiiiiiiiiiiiiiiiiiiiiiiiiiiiiiiiiiiiiiiiiiiiiiii iiiiiiiiiiiiiiiiiiiiiiiiiiiiiiii
Tuuuuuuuuuuuuuuuuuuuuuuuuuuuuuuuuuuuuuuuuuuuuuuuuuuuuuuuuuu uuuuuuuuuuuuuuuuuuuuu
Ze are ze buzzzzzzz Be are be buzzzzzzz Te are te buzzzzzzzzzzzzzzzzzzzzzzzzzz...

Zibin'tu is deforming. Zi, Bin, Tu. There is more than one snake gliding in the jar's fog. And is that—

A leaf?

How! And it's multiplying as you look.

Now there are snakes and leaves fogged inside the jar. Hissing, crinkling. And is that—

A giant bee?

How! And it's multiplying as you look.

Snakes, leaves and bees slithering, crackling, buzzing in the jar. And bells! They are pealing, tinkling, chiming, smashing inside the jar, inside your head. *Bzzzzzzz!* Rasping, humming, chattering, *bzzzzzzz!* Squeaking, piping, wailing, growling, roaring, prowling in the jar, in your head.

Bzzzzzzz!

At the peak of the dreadful noise, the jar throbbing and bouncing, your head impossibly loud, you think yourself—

50.

It's wet weather when you reach your home in Sector Z at the blush of New Inkululu's dusk. Your whole senses are overwhelmed with the awful thrumming of snakes, bees, leaves, bells and beasts in the jar, in your head that have accompanied you all this way here.

Mama is waiting for you, sat under the mopane tree in the rain. She is wearing a burnt-yellow, belly-bottomed onesie. It's as if she sensed you all along, knew you were coming. She speaks without turning. 'You were always gifted.'

'What a bonus for me,' you say, unable to hold back the hurt of her rejection. How she stepped into herself, then gave you away.

She looks at you, startled at your new sound, the husk in your words that now close with a scratch. How did she expect a torn, scarred tongue to sound? She recovers enough to say nothing of it.

Instead, she says, 'No, I mean it. You were always much gifted, chile.'

You're close to telling her about the casket and the tomb, what the Guardians did—asking, would it have happened without any abandoning? But no. You'll not be the one to enlighten her And, come to think of it, wasn't she... didn't she... ?

You sit beside her.

'Praise from you—am I hearing right, Mama? I want to ask but won't if it's cassava brew talking, that perhaps you might you have changed your position about imbibing.'

She laughs. 'I'm alright. Same, same, never a drinker.' She pauses for a moment. 'I must say you're both a shock and a delight for me.'

'Now?'

'You have always been.' There's pride in her voice.

Your heart swells to hear words you longed for but never heard, not from your mother before. She says nothing of your tattered clothing that Zibin'tu chewed and vomited, your near nakedness in rips.

'I guess I'm not as intolerant to learning as you thought, Mama.'

'No. You're not,' she says.

'You don't know how much you taught me, Mama.'

She takes your hand then, speaks, still without looking at you. 'I'm sorry about what they did to your tongue.' Finally, she will address it. 'It was my fault. What happened with Mau'aa.'

You pull your hand as if the touch of her nails polished in violet rain burns. 'How is it your fault?'

'You were always a mischievous one. I should have taught you to restrain your magic.'

'Mau'aa—'

'She was perfect for you,' Mama says.

'But I thought—'

'Never. A flower is a flower. It didn't matter that she was a girl. I should have done more for you. Saved you from yourself.'

'You were there,' you cry accusingly. 'You came to the tower. That was you! It was you, not a dream. And you were also there at the sound island!'

'Yes.'

'Why did you come to my prison?'

'Why do you think?' she says quietly.

'That you came to remind me of my power. How I could harness the spirit-light of Vuiili-ki and Vuiili-ku, the spirit moons of Wiimb-ó, to find my new self.'

'Chile, you're so ripe, I've been waiting for you to pop. You just needed a little nudge.'

'But why did you feel the need to help me?'

'Still you ask? I came to you in your time of need because I am your mother. You have my steadfast support. You will always have my support. What mother am I otherwise?'

'You let the Guardians take me.'

'I am sorry I was not there for you sooner,' she says again.

'Is that the only reason you're sorry?'

'I am sorry I refused to listen to Baba. He said I should train your magic to be more potent.'

'He kept you honest,' you say.

'He keeps us honest. Your new sound is a blessing—I hope you know that.'

'Mama.' You pause, unknowing how to say this. So you pull out the jar, quietly hold it out so she can see for herself the creatures forming and deforming in it.

She simply nods.

'They're not just in the jar,' you say. 'They are inside my head.'

Again, she nods.

'But how?' you ask.

'Chile, you insist to understand.' Her voice is soft, though you know she's scolding you.

You grip her arm. 'After all that's happened, is it not my right to know what lives inside me?'

'You've always known you're birthed of Susu Nunya, Raevaagi and Maadiregi stock. You have the blood of scholars and sorcerers, bards and Maadiregi—the gifted ones.'

'Why didn't you feel the Nga'phandileh talking inside my head, your own head? Why didn't Baba feel any of it?'

'You don't get much say in what chooses to live inside you.' She looks at you for a long time. 'Do you?' Her words are a whisper, full of burn. It's as though she doubts her own reasoning, that perhaps you chose.

'But *how* did the Nga'phandileh get free from the Hogiiri Hile Halah?'

She shrugs. 'I have no more answers than you. Maybe the silence of the sound island, coupled with spirit-light in the auras of Vuiili-ki and Vuiili-ku... Perhaps an innocent intent to free you from the sound island also created a deadly back door that released the Nga'phandileh?'

'Zie calls me master.'

'And why is that a surprise?'

'What are you saying, Mama?'

'Don't you know? When a duckling cracks from an egg and opens its eyes, it thinks the first thing it sees is its mother.'

'Even if it were a box?'

'Even if it were a box. It's a way for a thing that doesn't recognise itself to find identity, to form a bond with another thing and inherit its own meaning. I think that might be what happened with the Nga'phandileh.'

You ponder this awhile as you sit in comfortable silence together through the rain.

'There was a child with a basket,' you say unhappily.

Mama stares out in the horizon as if she hasn't heard. Then she tilts her head in a way that could be a nod, maybe not.

51.

You touch everything as if it's the last time you'll ever touch anything in your childhood home. Everything you remember from growing up, together with the newness, pulls tears.

'You're coming back, no?' Mama says.

You smile sadly, unknowing the answer.

You continue marking territory, putting arms around the mopane tree, then the tulip tree, squeezing life out of their trunks. You hug and kiss the walls of your late father's mansion as though they were lovers. You gaze at the black stone basin a long time, deciphering its tiered rock design, the sparkliest water cascading along its walls.

Much as you want to reminisce and trace the past, you don't ask Mama if she wants to watch a documentary with you in the home theatre—the markets, the home holos of you and Baba, how he nearly drowned you in a black river. You succumb to your hunger, and let Mama serve you steamed fish moist in banana leaves. She plates it on the great-grandfather sapele mahogany table stood from generation to generation. It's striated with grains of gold, and has six matching chairs in their natural beauty, no upholstery. Same wood as the doors of the house.

You notice a new burnt-clay bottle vase with yellow flowers on the table and think with sadness that Mama is moving on without you, without Baba. She watches across the table as you eat. Then she stands, clears the plate in your stead, reminding you that now you're a guest here. Where you belong is elsewhere.

'I want you to help me make a sweet crust,' she says.

'For a wild mango tart?'

'For any tart you like, but we can make it wild mango.'

You bite your tongue from suggesting durian rice pudding with miracle berry wine. It was Baba's favourite dessert, but never served inside a tart. You're not sure how well Mama can lever recollections of your father without stepping back again into herself. You don't know if she has recovered, although she's making a good show of it.

She doesn't take her eyes off you, it's as if she never will. She's leaning, elbows on the tabletop, face in her hands. You measure out granulated brown cane sugar, cream and flour into a bowl. You add a pinch of sea salt and crumble in some butter. You knead, just enough, so the dough's not too wet, too dry.

'Do you want to lick my hands?' you joke, and you laugh together. It reminds you of how Mama let you slurp the wooden spoon when she made cake or pancakes those days of your childhood.

'Will you make a ball of it now?' she asks.

'You taught me how best to do it.' You make a ball of the dough, then flatten it with your palm.

You let it rest.

'Good,' she says as if you were a child again. 'Wash your hands and help me make your bed.'

52.

Your room is just as you left it that late evening Hulor Mwe'ra and Hulor Kari'bu came to take you. The clothes are untouched in your wardrobe. But the bed is naked as if Mama hauled out your sheets but couldn't bring herself to replace them with clean ones.

She pulls out a drawer in the chiffonier and lifts out a bright-yellow fitted sheet with bright-red baby tulips on it.

'That's a bit too sunny,' you protest.

'You used to like it.'

'When I was little, Mama.'

Together, you stretch the fitted sheet over the mattress, tuck the bottoms and sides. You drape a coverlet and fold it back at the head. You toss a quilt on top, then case matching pillows and pat them smooth.

Back in the kitchen, the dough is well rested. You sprinkle flour on the clean bench and flatten the dough with a rolling pin without it sticking. You arrange it in a baking tray, let it overflow and pinch the sides for pattern, then you bake it in the oven until it's golden brown.

'We'll let it cool now,' you say to nobody in particular, as if you're reminding yourself of family. You're keen to spend more time with Mama, yet it's all so confusing. That you're here, that Mama is here, that she is not stepped in and aloof but is rather outward-reaching toward you. You pile on together layers of custard and wild mango puree from her home-made jars in the cooler, your hands every now and then touching.

Without warning, she throws herself at you, hugs you as if she's smelling you, as if you will dissolve if she lets go of you. She clings, almost waiting for you to disengage first.

'I am not going to push you away,' you speak to her neck.

She nods, lets go.

'There's a slice of a tart I made before,' she says, tears shining in her eyes.

'Yes. Please.' A hot invisible potato sears your throat.

You cool the aching of memory with a taste of home. You linger in your tongue the flavour of sweet milk and butter on your mother's tart. You see Baba, imagine him at the head of the table. How sometimes he would let you arrange the placemats, then he disarranged them. You'd set the table with steaming bowls that smelled like a feast, even though they were simply broiled fowl served with clove-seed rice, or coriander-stewed plantains on a bed of thrice-cooked, dried, then stir-fried baby pumpkin leaves pan-tossed in the whitest coconut milk. Then Baba would disarrange your careful array, mislay your plate and put you at the head of the table instead of him.

'So you may learn to take care of others,' he said, the first time you looked up in confusion, brow furled.

You miss his kind face, the firmness of his hands pressed together close to his nose as he said grace. 'The World came whole, the World became whole.'

'The World came whole, the World became whole,' you and Mama answered in prayer.

Baba taught you the manners with which to eat food. 'We chew mouth closed.'

Mama didn't put it as politely. 'Nobody needs to see all the shit going on in the middle of your mouth. Leave that for the crapper.'

Now you take a sizzling shower inside the crystal-powered bathroom in the adjoining twin shells, the one where you sleep on the other side of the shelled dome that houses the lounge and dining room.

'I am going to burn these,' you hear Mama say of your foul rags scattered on the corridor. 'They are revolting.'

You come out dripping wet, and Mama is there for you. She wraps you with a soft black towel. Redressed in night wear, you let her tuck you in the soft sheets of your old bed.

'His smile was big,' you say.

'Wasn't it, just?' Her face is wet with tears you have not seen much since Baba died.

'Is he—'

'In Eh'wauizo, yes. The place of our ancestors.'

It consoles you even a little that he's in a place he can reach you, although he hasn't tried to yet, and this pains you.

A roar, and bigger rain falls hard outside.

53.

*Ziiiiiiiiiiiiiiiiiiiiiiiiiiiiiiiiiiiiiiiiiiiiiiiiiiiiiiiiiiiiiiiiiiiiiiiiiiiiiiiiiiiiiiiiiiiiiiiii
iiiiiiiiiiiiiiiiiiiiiiiiiiiiiiiii
biiiiiiiiiiiiiiiiiiiiiiiiiiiiiiiiiiiiiiiiiiiiiiiiiiiiiiiiiiiiiiiiiiiiiiiiiiiiiiiiiiiiiiiiiiiiiiiiiiiiiii
iiiiiiiiiiiiiiiiiiiiiiiiiiiiiiiii
tuuuuuuuuuuuuuuuuuuuuuuuuuuuuuuuuuuuuuuuuuuuuuuuuuuuuuuuuuuuuuu
uuuuuuuuuuuuuuuuuuuuu
Ze are ze buzzzzzzzzzzzzzzzzzzzzzzz...*

Zibin'tu is deforming more. Zie's further from hir form that was once
Zi, Bin, Tu.

The snakes, the leaves, the bees, the bells and the fog in the jar, in
your head.

It's a new dawn, the suns not out yet, and already you miss the
home you haven't yet left one more time, and this time you'll
abandon it of your own volition. You're in fresh, new garments, ready
for an ordeal.

Is anything more heart-wrenching like breakfast your mother has
made?

Mama cracks eggs with her hands in that special way. Fries them
together with a sliver of sundried nguwe'we, horned boar from the
market. She serves the eggs exactly how you like them, sunny-side
up, drizzled with sizzling oil on its face. The yolk is firm but oozy,
weeping into home-fresh coconut bread. How well will you eat like
this again?

Finally, you both know it is time.

'You can take anything you want from this house,' Mama offers.
'Take it with you. Anything.'

You shake your head. Guardians do not want, they lack for
nothing. Mama knows this. That is why she does not insist. She puts
out a hand for you.

'Come.' Holds you as if you were a child all over again, as if
reinventing you to fit her world more this time.

You wrap your bigger fingers around hers.

In your other hand is the bucking jar with its slithering snakes and cracking leaves and buzzing bees and ringing bells and splitting fog. You let Mama walk you to the gate.

'I don't want to go,' you say.

'I know this. Yet it's something you must do, Chant'L.' Your name slips like an endearment from Mama's lips.

'Yes.'

'Wait,' she says as you turn. 'I can do one small thing. Put the jar in my hands, let's hold it together.' Her chant is soft, the sound smooth as the feathers of a baby bird. 'She was the first to see the Word. Khwa'ra.'

'It is acquired,' you say.

'Ya'yn.'

'It is uttered,' you say.

'Ra'kwa.'

'It is released,' you say.

She hands back the jar.

'Mama.'

'Yes?'

'I have never seen you—'

'Practice magic like this?'

'Yes.'

'You know that saying about two heads being better than one.'

'Yes, or empty vessels making the loudest noise. I guess your silence speaks to the richness of your vessel.'

'Our magic will only hold them for a moment longer,' she says. 'You're already clear about what must be done, I don't have to tell you.'

'I must put them back inside the wall.'

'That. Yes.'

54.

Ziiiiiiiiiiiiiiiiiiiiiiiiiiiiiiiiiiiiiiiiiiiiiiiiiiiiiiiiiiiiiiiiiiiiiiiiiiiiiiiiiiiiiiiiiiiii iiiiiiiiiiiiiiiiiiiiiiiiiiiiii
biiiiiiiiiiiiiiiiiiiiiiiiiiiiiiiiiiiiiiiiiiiiiiiiiiiiiiiiiiiiiiiiiiiiiiiiiiiiiiiiiiiiiiiiiiiiiiii iiiiiiiiiiiiiiiiiiiiiiiiiiiiiiii
tuuuuuuuuuuuuuuuuuuuuuuuuuuuuuuuuuuuuuuuuuuuuuuuuuuuuuuuuuuuuuuuuu uuuuuuuuuuuuuuuuuuuuuu
Ze are ze ze buzzzzzzzzzzzzzzzzzzzzzzzz...

You don't need a shuttle with a smooth nose and a tapered body to lift for the skies and take you to your destination. You have no wish for Hulor Mwe'ra behind the wheel steering you to the tower, he'd deliberately crash you both.

You think yourself to the courtyard and its flow and movement everywhere, height and angles, ovals and domes. You feel strangely at home with the motion and urgency, the sensors and silhouettes, movements and lights of the place you came to know as home away from home. What do you feel with this homecoming? You can't really say. You're misplaced in this world, yet you belong.

You take the steps, too many of them, leading from the courtyard. You could have taken the lift, a smooth glide up, your stomach falling until it doesn't. You could have thought yourself up, easy, but where's the fun in that? Your tongue is healed, your sound magic restored, more potent with spirit-light...

You do it the hard way.

You climb with the resolution of an executioner, up, up the ancient stone stairs, natural boulders sculptured all the way to the clouds. You touch the hand-carved chapel door embossed with portals to the gods on polished blackwood, and pause for a moment.

It's a heavy door and you push it with the weight of a lifetime.

55.

You enter the chapel where the Guardians are in prayer.

They are knelt in supplication, and startle at your approach.

'What madness—?' begins Hulor Mwe'ra, half-rising. His glare suggests his mind is stewing with a search for the right colourful language that might, in his infuriation, apply to you:

Foul aborted liver of a malnourished inka-inka!

Smelly regurgitate of a glutenous p'hobawawa!

Not quite the reunion you were hoping to get.

'Your glee to see me,' you can't resist prodding him despite his already excitable state.

You cannot help but notice how Hulor Kari'bu winces at your disembodied voice—how it's broken from the sweet sound of running water to this one mottled with scratch. Is it surprising that it's only Kari'bu who seems to notice, not the rest of the Guardians? No.

'Irony will get you nowhere.' Hulor Mwe'ra leaps to his feet, now he will crush you. There's a dance of blue and red fire in his eyes.

But Kari'bu holds him back with a touch. 'Have we not done enough?'

'And I'll stand by it!' says Mwe'ra.

'Let's hear what the chile has to say.' Kari'bu's insistence is gentle.

'How can we give ears to one who refuses to listen?' snaps Hulor Nd'ani.

'No one is relinquishing anything,' says Jin in the most sober voice you've ever heard from them.

Pita makes a sound, says nothing for a moment. Then: 'How did you get out of the soundless prison?'

'Don't bring it up,' you say. 'We all make mistakes, but what you did—it's still a sore matter.'

'Perhaps we were just shoddy in our magic,' says Mwe'ra. 'We'll do it better this time.'

'That's so great.' You mimic him, speaking with a madness or confidence that surprises even you. 'Mwe'ra—' you call him by name, and he's just about spluttering, 'you seem very attached to this punishing thing. Try another crack at it, see what happens. Mmhh?'

Truth is, for the first time, you pity Mwe'ra, shapeless as he is with age, blackened with the absence of what he can be. Where, when can he find his true potential? You're uncertain he's the best teacher for you.

Hulor Mwe'ra sees the jar you're holding, and falls back. He points at the omen in your clutch. 'What have you *done*?'

'Would you imagine? I've gripped the beast as much as it has gripped me,' you say.

Hulor Jin is agitated, throwing their arms. They trip on their feet and collapse in a heap.

'Then we'll put you right back in the sound island where you should have stayed!' shouts Mwe'ra.

'You don't want to do that.' You hold out the jar full of snakes and bees and leaves and bells and beasts. 'But you're welcome to try it.'

'How—?' says Hulor Kari'bu.

'Precisely,' you say.

Hulor Jin is back on their feet, brushing themselves, a little sober again.

Ziiiiiiiiiiiiiiiiiiiiiiiiiiiiiiiiiiiiiiiiiiiiiiiiiiiiiiiiiiiiiiiiiiiiiiiiiiiiiiiiiiiiiiiiiiiiiiiiiiiiiiiiiiii iiiiiiiiiiiiiiiiiiiiiiiiiiiiiiiiii

biiiiiiiiiiiiiiiiiiiiiiiiiiiiiiiiiiiiiiiiiiiiiiiiiiiiiiiiiiiiiiiiiiiiiiiiiiiiiiiiiiiiiiiiiiiiiiiiiiiiiiiiiiii iiiiiiiiiiiiiiiiiiiiiiiiiiiiiiiiiiiiii

tuuuuuuuuuuuuuuuuuuuuuuuuuuuuuuuuuuuuuuuuuuuuuuuuuuuuuuuuuu uuuuuuuuuuuuuuuuuuuuuuuu

Ze are ze ze buzzzzzzzzzzzzzzzzzzzzzzzzz.

The snakes and bees and leaves and bells and beasts are writhing and jumping and scratching and clinging and howling terribly. It's as if there's a bigger space inside the jar than meets the naked eye.

Doggedly, you look at the Guardians. 'Truce? Let's just say we need each other.'

56.

ziiiiiiiiiiiiiiiiiiiiiiiiiiiiiiiiiiiiiiiiiiiiiiiiiiiiiiiiiiiiiiiiiiiiiiiiiiiiiiiiiiiiiiiiiiiiiiii iiiiiiiiiiiiiiiiiiiiiiiiiii
biiiiiiiiiiiiiiiiiiiiiiiiiiiiiiiiiiiiiiiiiiiiiiiiiiiiiiiiiiiiiiiiiiiiiiiiiiiiiiiiiiiiiiiiiiiiiiiiiiiiiii iiiiiiiiiiiiiiiiiiiiiiiiiiiii
tuuuuuuuuuuuuuuuuuuuuuuuuuuuuuuuuuuuuuuuuuuuuuuuuuuuuuuuuuuuuu uuuuuuuuuuuuuuuuuuuuu

The Nga'phandileh is once more a hive mind. Fully deformed.

An eternal buzzzzzzzzzzzzzzzzzzzzzzzz...

Khwa'ra. It is acquired.
Ya'yn. It is uttered.
Ra'kwa. It is released.

Your magic is the sound of a hot-headed river rushing over a crag in a monstrous waterfall. It is done. The people of Sector Z, New Inku'lulu, the whole of Zezépfeni and the rest of the planets are safe. Ekwukwe, Orino-Rin, Wiimb-ó and Pinaa—all protected from the destructive nature of the Nga'phandileh one more time.

But for how long? As long as it takes.

You can't help but wonder about Zibin'tu and quickly dismiss hir from your mind. A Ramarire council need not know about this matter. It's between you and the Guardians.

And the Nga'phandileh.

'What about Mau'aa?' you ask the ineffable. You try not to sound unselfish. The remorse you still feel is honest but things must be tackled, then put to rest. 'What will we tell the people of Sector Z?'

The Guardians look at you. They can't be serious! The arrogance of these people! Mwe'ra. Kari'bu. Nd'ani. Pita. Jin. They are the Guardians who made you. Guardians who destroyed you. Guardians deconstructing you.

Together, you are the Guardians. What you do is protect. You keep people safe.

Hulor Kari'bu smiles encouragement. She's still unaccustomed to your voice that is removed from itself. Hulor Mwe'ra's eyes are promising with much certainty that your time in the tower, whatever time remains, you will regret it. Hulor Pita, generally without choosing a side, is now pouting, his lips full of fate—yours, or his? Hulor Nd'ani is angrier than you've ever seen her, she could well throw a fist and it will hurt the same. Hulor Jin is cockeyed on the wings, undoubtedly harbouring thoughts about how the sooner you get this done, the sooner they can clutch a gourd of yummily brew.

You're the youngest, the fastest—they know this.

They *know*.

It creates an opportunity, and this time you welcome it. Hulor Kari'bu hands you the blowing horn. 'Go on. Do it, Chant'L.'

Your fingers brush as, resolutely, you clasp the horn.

Epilogue

*ziiiiiiiiiiiiiiiiiiiiiiiiiiiiiiiiiiiiiiiiiiiiiiiiiiiiiiiiiiiiiiiiiiiiiiiiiiiiiiiiiiiiiiiiiiiiiiiiiiii
iiiiiiiiiiiiiiiiiiiiiiiii*
*biiiiiiiiiiiiiiiiiiiiiiiiiiiiiiiiiiiiiiiiiiiiiiiiiiiiiiiiiiiiiiiiiiiiiiiiiiiiiiiiiiiiiiiiiiiiiiiiiiii
iiiiiiiiiiiiiiiiiiiiiiiiiii*
*tuuuuuuuuuuuuuuuuuuuuuuuuuuuuuuuuuuuuuuuuuuuuuuuuuuuuuuuuuuuuuuu
uuuuuuuuuuuuuuuuuuuuuu*

Zibin'tu is back in hir hive mind. Hirs is yet again the sound of incoherence, a mindless multiplicity of howling trapped inside the wall that offers, that takes. An eternal—

Buzzzzzzzzzzzzzzzzzzzzzzzz... The Hogiiri Hile Halah takes more than it gives.

The pulse inside the wall is calling to you. You lean your ear towards the luring. A gorging want that draws you close, closer. Buzzzzzzzzzzzzzzzzzzzzzzzzz. It's the layered buzz of a jillion hearts zinging in echo entrapped within the wall. So soft its calling, it nudges you to step forward, to listen, please listen the sound willing you with a gobbling need to touch it.

Touch the wall, please touch the wall. A surge of unbeatable desire unravels your being.

Just then, the air fills with the music of a magic whistle you'd know anywhere. It's the clearest you've ever heard it, and its gentle toot refrains you from touching the dastardly wall.

Baba is here, saving you from yourself. *Now. You. See—*

There he is in white mist straight from Eh'wauizo. His kindly face, his chestnut eyes.

> He's fading in and out,
> clasping his stomach
> and inviting you
> to the merry peal
> of his purest
> laughter.

Glossary

Terminology (and names) drawn from Swahili, Afrocentric or made-up language

Creatures

Name	Description/derivation	English pronunciation
aze'aze	made-up word: giant firefly with the head of a goat	*a-zay-a-zay*
chekele'le	hyena, derived from 'cheka'—it means laugh in Swahili	*check-e-ley-ley*
dragon-no	dragon	*drag-on-no*
impudu-pudu	derived from the impundulu, a mythical lightning bird in African folklore	*imp-poo-doo-poo-doo*
inka-inka	made-up creature	*ink-a-ink-a*
mamba'ba	mamba, giant snake	*mam-ba-ba*
ndege'ndege	ostrich, derived from 'ndege'—it means bird in Swahili	*n-de-ge-n-de-ge*
Nga'phandileh	creatures of unreality	*n-gaa-pha-n-dee-ley*
nguwe'we	horned pig, derived from 'nguruwe'	*n-goo-way-way*
p'hobawawa	one-eyed bat, derived from mythical African beast popobawa	*po-po-ba-wa*
t'embo'oo	elephant, derived from 'tembo' in Swahili	*t-eh-m-bo-o-o*
tikolokolo	made-up, spirit gremlin	*tee-koh-loh-koh-loh*
Zibin'tu	derived from bintu, anomalous plural of 'mtu', Swahili for person; also a fabled term for a bad spirit	*Zee-bin-too*

Gemstones

Name	Description/derivation	Pronunciation
d'hiamomo	diamond	*die-aa-mow-mow*
rhorhodolite	rhodolite	*rho-rho-doh-light*
t'lazanini	tanzanite	*t-lah-zah-nee-nee*
t'sasavorite	tsavorite	*t-sir-sir-voh-right*

Objects

Name	Description/derivation	English pronunciation
k'hora'aa	kora, African musical instrument	*kho-rah-aa*
luhte'te	lute, African musical instrument	*loot-e-tey*

Other terminology

Name	Description/derivation	*Pronunciation*
Boāmmariri	conference of planets held every five years	*Bow-ahm-mah-ree-ree*
Hogiiri Hile Halah	Wall protecting the system from the Nga'phandileh, creatures of unreality	*Hoo-ghee-ree Hee-ley Hah-lah*
khwa'ra	to seed, conceive, receive	*k-wah-rah*
o'livha'vha	olive	*oh-lee-vah-vha*
ra'kwa	offspring	*rah-k-waa*
ya'yn	mother	*yah-ii-nn*

People

Name	Description/derivation	English pronunciation
Chant'L	derived from 'chant', **she/her**	*Shan-tell*
Hulor	made up title for guardians and jurors who secure the Hogiiri Hile Halah, the protective wall from the Nga'phandileh threat.	*Hoo('oo' as in look)-loh-rr*
Jin	derived from jin/djinn/ jini, **they/them**	*J-een*
Kari'bu	it means 'welcome', derived from 'karibu' in Swahili, **she/her**	
Mau'aa	it means 'flowers', derived from 'maua' in Swahili, **she/her**	*Mah-oo-ah ('oo' as in look)*
Mkha'lingalinga	derived from Malinga, an African name that means 'brave' or 'tolerance', **she/her**	*M-kaa-lee-ngaa-lee-ngaa*
Mwe'ra	made up name, **he/him**	*M-way-rah / M-weh-rah*
Nd'ani,	it means 'inside', derived from 'ndani' in Swahili, **she/her**	*N-dah-nee*
Pita	it means 'pass', derived from 'pita' in Swahili, **he/him**	*Pee-tah*

Planets and places

Name	Description/derivation	English pronunciation
Ekwukwe	echo planet, from the Igbo word 'ukwe' which means 'song' or 'anthem'	*Eh-kwoo-kweh*
New Inku'lulu	an elite Zezépfeni look-alike space outpost	*New Ink-oo(as in 'look')-loo-loo*
Órino-Rin	gas giant planet with sonic storms, from the Yoruba word 'orin', which means 'song'	*Oh-reen-oh-reen*
Pinaa	inhabited moon, from the Setswana word 'pina', which means 'song'	*Pee-nah*
Sector Z	an echo spire in New Inku'lulu—here, the Guardians protect citizens from the Nga'phandileh threat	
Wiimb-ó	Earth-analogue planet, from the Swahili word 'wimbo', which means 'song'	*Wee-m-boh*
Zezépfeni	elite planet of the 'original race', from the Amharic word 'zefeni', which means 'song'	*Zey-zey-fey-nee*

Trades

Name	Description/derivation	English pronunciation
Maadiregi	tradesperson/professional e.g. engineer, technician, architect	*Ma-aa-dee-rey-ghee*
Mahadum	institution of learning, derived from Igbo word for university	*Mah-ha-doom*
Raevaagi	bearer of history, a messenger, bard, storyteller, orator	*Rah-ey-vaa-ghee*
Ramarire	distinguished council of jurors in the planet of Zezépfeni, privy to knowledge of the Nga'phandileh, the beings of unreality	*Rah-mah-ree-reh*
Susu Nunyaa	elite order tasked with interpreting lost language	*Soo-soo-noo-n-yaa*
Taq'qerara	special born and gifted with the magic to feel sound aura	*Tak-keh-rah-rah*
Uroh-gi	healer	*Oo-roh-ghee ('oo' as in 'look'*

| Zéhemgwile | guild of tailors | *Zey-hey-m-g-wee-ley* |

Also by Eugen Bacon

Fiction

- Novic
- A Place Between Waking and Forgetting
- Secondhand Daylight (with Andrew Hook)
- Languages of Water (ed)—cross-lingual hybrid
- Serengotti
- Broken Paradise
- Chasing Whispers
- Mage of Fools
- Danged Black Thing
- The Road to Woop Woop & Other Stories
- Ivory's Story
- Hadithi & The State of Black Speculative Fiction (with Milton Davis)
- Claiming T-Mo

Poetry

- Texture of Silence (with Steve Simpson)
- Saving Shadows
- Speculate (with Dominique Hecq)
- Black Moon: Graphic Speculative Flash Fiction

Non-Fiction

- Afro-Centered Futurisms in Our Speculative Fiction
- An Earnest Blackness
- Writing Speculative Fiction

About the Author

Eugen Bacon is an African Australian author. She's a Solstice, British Fantasy, Locus and Foreword Indies Award winner, a twice World Fantasy and Shirley Jackson Award finalist, and a finalist in the Philip K. Dick and Ignyte Awards, and the Nommo Awards for speculative fiction by Africans. Eugen is an Otherwise Fellow, and was also announced in the honor list for 'doing exciting work in gender and speculative fiction'. *Danged Black Thing* made the Otherwise Award Honor List as a 'sharp collection of Afro-Surrealist work'. Visit her at eugenbacon.com.